Stephen Rowley was born and lived in Belfast until 1972. In Belfast, he attended Annadale Grammar School. After a BA from Essex University (1975), he was awarded a PhD by Manchester University (1979). Stephen's other degrees are: PGCE in TESOL (London University; *Maîtrise* (Bordeaux University) and *Habilitation* (Paris University). He was appointed Professor of English at Artois University (France) in 2008 where he worked as Vice-President (International Affairs) for five years. Stephen was then recruited by the prestigious Sun Yat-sen University, China, as part of the '100 Talents Programme' and became Director of the European Centre there. He edited and wrote an introduction to *European Perceptions of China and Perspectives on the Belt and Road Initiative* (Brill, 2021) as well as writing more than 60 academic artices published in journals in the UK, US, France, Italy and China, and several works of fiction and poetry.

To my mother.

And her mother, who came from the other side.

Stephen Rowley

THE WOMAN FROM THE OTHER SIDE

The Belfast Stories

AUSTIN MACAULEY PUBLISHERS™

LONDON • CAMBRIDGE • NEW YORK • SHARJAH

A CIP catalogue record for this title is available from the British Library.

ISBN 9781035816026 (Paperback)
ISBN 9781035816033 (ePub e-book)

www.austinmacauley.com

First Published 2023
Austin Macauley Publishers Ltd®
1 Canada Square
Canary Wharf
London
E14 5AA

I would like to thank Clive Lee and Cornelius Crowley.
Ever the best of friends.

Table of Contents

The Woman from the Other Side

Mary O'Brien was born in County Cavan at the end of the First World War. She was the last of eleven children and her father was happy to see her married just before the Second World War began, even though it was to a Belfast protestant the family had met on holiday in Omeath. Mary did not realise just how 'staunch' a protestant her future husband was until well after he asked her nicely to change her religion and come to live with him at the top end of Belfast's Donegall Pass. After the wedding, Mary would not see her family again for many years, and when she did it was because her closest sister came to Belfast for the weekend and they met briefly in town for tea. Neither would she see the inside of a Catholic church for an even longer period. Her three children, all boys—were brought up in the protestant faith and knew nothing of their mother's 'persuasion' which the father constantly referred to as pure superstition that was closer to pagan fetishism than to any true religion. The children grew up believing that the 'other side' were not quite human and they would not have been surprised to be told that a certain amount of cannibalism occurred during Catholic rituals. At all costs, the 'other side' were to be avoided—which was not difficult in the 1940s and 50s due to Belfast's segregated educational system.

Before they had met, and during the early years of their marriage, the husband, William McCauley—had worked in the shipyard, but unfortunately, he had a strong penchant for 'the demon drink' as everyone called it. He kept a slate in two pubs but once, when his bills became too high and impossible to pay off on his worker's salary, he ran off and went 'on the boats' like many others in a similar predicament. He wrote each month to his wife and sent her enough money to live on, along with instructions that she was to tell anyone who came to the house that William would be back shortly and would pay off the remainder of his debts, like the honest man he felt himself to be. This solution of running up debts and then going on the boats for several months, became a pattern which William embraced for the rest of his working life. Ironically, it was the sea which provided him with the circumstances to 'dry out', albeit temporarily.

In 1957, William McCauley went on the boats for the last time—a Canadian merchant navy ship known as the Nellie. He had amassed considerable debts at both of his regular pubs and even his wife acknowledged that it would be in the family's interest if her husband were to go to sea for a while. The boys were growing up and had part-time jobs in local shops and chippies, so there was less pressure on finding money to put bread on the table. When called upon, William's mother made the house repayments.

For the first couple of months, things went relatively to plan and Mary received money from her husband. Then, in the middle of the third month she received a letter signed by the captain of the Nellie, on what appeared to be official notepaper and which stated the following:

Of course, Mary was shocked by this information and stunned by the implicit repercussions that it would now have upon her life. The love that she had felt for her husband when she married him had evolved into a life of marital duty and self-abnegation which was almost free of emotion. She was not overwhelmed by sorrow. In fact, her immediate concern was that the sum of money she would receive would be sufficient to pay off her husband's remaining debts. Her boys could now fend for themselves and the eldest, William was already talking about marriage. Mary herself was but in her early forties and her children and daily household tasks had kept her in good shape. She was not one for sitting too long in a chair. It was with a certain pride and confidence that she looked at her figure in the mirror. She could perhaps contemplate returning to the 'true faith' one day and maybe even visit her family in Cavan. The notion that the future might seem rosier than the past made her feel uneasy and slightly ashamed but the clouds did appear to possess at least a thin, silver lining.

Mary was disappointed by the sum she received from the merchant navy. It was enough to cover just over half what her husband owed and she was obliged to work in a linen mill nearby in order to pay off the rest and then take the mortgage payments upon herself. It took her almost two years to complete the former and she celebrated the end of the payments by visiting a nearby Catholic church and giving thanks. She went to great pains to ensure that no one saw her enter Saint Malachy's Parish and when she was there, she spoke to no one. She stood in awe of the fan vaulted ceiling and felt a burden finally drop from her shoulders. She also felt spiritually restored for the first time in decades. Mary lit a candle for her deceased husband and prayed for his soul. This was the start of cherished, but discreet weekly visits to the Parish.

As the years went by, her sons married and moved to other parts of Belfast. Mary was not lonely as she had friends from work and neighbours who would drop in for a cup of tea. With them, she remained vague about her religious past, saying only that she was a country girl from outside Belfast. She continued to visit St. Malachy's where she would now frequently attend mass. To the women she came into contact with she was known as Mary O'Brien from Cavan, keeping her present circumstances vague. Another parishioner once claimed that she knew the O'Briens from Cavan but Mary passed it off with a quip about there being more O'Briens in Ireland than there are lampposts. Still, her double identity began to weigh increasingly upon her as time went by.

Then, an event took place which changed Mary's life and made the routine she had set in place impossible to keep to. She had now spent much more of her life with her Protestant family in Belfast than in her Catholic childhood home and was just about managing to hold both threads of her life together. Her husband had been dead now for almost six years and the widow was still not fifty. She felt full of energy and wanted to contribute to both church and community and when the priest at St Malachy's asked her to join a ladies' group which made home visits to the elderly and poor at weekends, Mary decided it was time to participate fully in life again. It was on one such visit that she met Sean Donahue, a widower like herself who lived with his elderly, invalid mother. He was nearing sixty and there was an instant attraction and complicity between them. Part of the attraction was undoubtedly a feeling of subdued mystery which surrounded both of them and encouraged the other to discover more.

The two began to make short visits to the local pub where Mary would take a wee sherry and Sean a Guinness. Despite his age, Sean did not like to drink alcohol in front of his mother. It was on one such outing that Sean confessed to Mary that he had been a member of a clandestine movement which had been involved in smuggling items into the country, but that she must not worry as he was past that sort of thing now. Recently, there had been disturbances in several parts of Belfast but thankfully, he was no longer needed. He felt better when he had got this secret off his chest and his warm smile moved Mary to tell him about her own circumstances and how she had left Cavan to live as a Protestant in the Donegall Pass. She confessed to renouncing the Catholic church for a number of years and that having rediscovered her faith, she had been faced with new problems. She told him about her sons and the two grandchildren who had recently come on the scene. Sean was both kind and understanding and when they parted that evening, he bent over and kissed her gently, amidst the dark which now shrouded the city.

For Mary, her confession to Sean marked a point of no return. Their relationship was deepening and strengthening so that both recognised that a commitment would have to be made. A confession would also have to be made to her boys. She decided to do the latter in two stages: on the first occasion she would tell them that she had met someone and that he was a Catholic. The boys would not take this well but she thought that they would come to terms with the issue eventually. The second stage would involve her telling them that she was a Catholic now and in fact had always been a Catholic. This would be much harder for them and at this point, Mary did not want to think about the consequences.

Sean and Mary decided to live together. They would marry, if the church would not oppose their marriage. Seven years had now passed since William's disappearance at sea which meant that there was no legal barrier to a marital contract.

Mary invited her sons for tea, telling them she had something important to share with them. They deduced correctly that it was about her meeting another man and they had no problems with this. When she told them that the other man was a Catholic, the three reacted in the same way and she felt that an enormous rift had suddenly opened up between herself and her sons. The boys left that evening by kissing their mother gently on the cheek and wishing her happiness but they were also resolved never to meet this 'Sean fella'.

She would have to spare them that affront and maintain a distant relationship.

Months passed before Mary resolved on their second meeting. She again invited them for the evening meal, hoping they would accept to meet Sean on the same occasion. She was met by staunch opposition and quickly accepted their refusal. The sons were convinced that the reason for this second meeting was to be informed of their mother's marriage and conversion to Catholicism. They braced themselves for the worst.

The boys sat down at the table and Mary poured them a glass of stout each. She began by telling them about her family in Cavan before coming to the really important piece of information:

"I was born and brought up Catholic so, in fact… I will not be converting to Catholicism in marrying Sean because I have always been a Catholic."

The boys were flabbergasted. They sat in silence, exchanging knowing glances but not looking at their mother until William finally decided to speak:

"Yer tellin' us nigh that yer a Catholic an' always have been a Catholic… ya know my name is William McCauley. I am the son of William McCauley who was also the son of William McCauley and all three generations have been proud members of the same Loyal Orange Lodge, sworn volunteers who will defend the faith and this wee country of ours… how d'ya think it looks to have a Catholic mother? I'm sorry, Ma, but I'll not be in this house again."

William rose and left the house without another word. His two brothers followed him in silence, leaving their mother alone at the table with their untouched glasses of stout. She had anticipated a very difficult moment with her boys but had never believed that they would abandon her in silence and that she would, to all intents and purposes, and for the second time in her life, be excluded from her family. She put her arms on the table and wept sorely.

Mary delayed her wedding with Sean (which was to be a purely civil affair in order to avoid any 'complications' with the church and its parishioners) for she remained in the hope that her boys would have a change of heart and even bring her grandchildren down for her to hug. She was wrong. As the sixties advanced, the rift between communities deepened and became more venomous until there was open warfare at the end of the decade. Mary and Sean kept separate houses but still fully intended to be married and live together as soon as circumstances would allow them to do so.

One morning, as Mary was hoovering the sitting-room, a knock came to the front door and when she opened it, she was confronted by William McCauley—the second of that name. It was Mary's turn to be in a state of shock but she managed to usher him in before collapsing into her armchair. It had now been more than eight years since this ghost had been lost at sea.

As Mary stared at him fixedly and in disbelief, William calmly told the story of how he had convinced one of his friends to steal a sheet of notepaper from the captain's desk and write the letter announcing his disappearance. It was posted from Canada, a country where William had taken up abode, even becoming a citizen. He decided to come 'home' because he had fallen down stairs and was now facing reduced mobility. She had not noticed his limp as he entered the sitting-room.

"Ya mean, ya came home to be nursed… so that I would nurse ya!" After the initial shock, Mary was in no mood to feel sorry for this man.

"I suppose ya could say that. After all, yar my wife an' it's yar duty."

Mary looked at him in total disbelief but before she could say anything, William continued:

"I came here yesterday but there was no one in. The neighbours told me where William lives so I spent last night in his house. He told me all about you and this Seamus fella. Hear yar getting married! Quite a turn up for the books, that one!"

Mary is again shell-shocked by the man's words. She can no longer even look at him.

"His name's Sean, not Seamus."

"Sean it is. But ya can't do that, ya know. Ya would be a bigamist!"

Mary's blood ran cold on hearing this word and she felt a wave of nausea sweeping over her. She looked at William and realised that he had come prepared for this day. He knew what he wanted and showed no sign of remorse or shame in what he had done. She felt she could have killed him at that point.

"You think you are goin' to live here—with me, in this house?"

"Aye, a do! My mother put down the deposit for this house an' it's in my name."

"Who d'ya think paid it off for the last eight years?"

"To be honest, that's a bit beside the point. I'm the legal owner… but you are most welcome to stay wi' me but we can't have any Taigs runnin' around the place—know whata mean?"

Mary knew very well what he meant. She had instantly made her mind up on the course of action to take as it was impossible to stay any longer with this obnoxious foreigner. She would move out today and come back another time for the rest of her belongings. The furniture was of little importance to her.

Mary moved in with Sean who had a house close to St Malachy's. At the beginning, she looked after the elderly mother but the latter died after only a month and the couple were faced with a dilemma as they were not, and could not be, married. Regrettably, the only solution would be to leave Belfast.

Sean sold his house and the couple moved to the Donegal side of Derry where they bought a modest home and had money left over for retirement, which Sean generously put on Mary's bank account. They lived a secluded life until Sean's death in 1972 when Mary went south again to live with her closest sister, Josie, who had moved to Sligo to spend her days gazing wistfully across the Atlantic. Josie had remained a spinster and was happy to have a bit of company in her later years. Mary never saw her sons or grandchildren again.

Time had a surprising effect upon her for she became bitter, unforgiving and resentful, instead of living her final years in relative peace, which would have been more in conformity with her former self. It seemed to Mary that her life had been a series of displacements which meant that she had never really been allowed to put down roots of her own. As a consequence of her feeling of estrangement, one day, Mary wrote to a Belfast newspaper relating the story of her husband who had deceived her, adding a copy of the letter his friend had sent announcing his death at sea. She wanted to publicly denounce him and the shameful deception which had destroyed her life and forced her once again to leave her home. But Mary did not know that, just before the publication of her story and letter in the newspaper, William had died in the presence of his sons and grandchildren, leaving their mother and grandmother a widow for the second time. Fortunately, Mary never discovered that she had the dubious distinction of twice being declared a widow to the same man.

The Sisters

Linda and Shirley Davies had lived all their lives together in Sandy Row until the former got married and bought a three-bedroomed house up the Donegall Road with her new husband, Michael. Today it was Shirley's turn to marry and the two young women sat drinking tea on the Saturday morning of the wedding which was to take place at the Saint Mary Magdalene Church of Ireland in the Donegall Pass. All the women of the family had been married in the same church whilst the boys married in the church their brides' families had attended. That was the way it happened in 1960s Belfast.

Linda put her cup on the saucer balanced on the arm of her chair.

"Listen, I have to be honest with ya, but I never thought James was the right one for you."

"Sure none of ya think he is!" Linda did not give her reason for making her remark but Shirley knew what she thought.

"It's not a question of not being good enough for ya—anyone's good enough when ya look at this dump!" her eyes perused the family home.

"Ya know what I mean?" What Linda in fact meant was that her sister would be marrying into the same: she and James would move into similar rented accommodation in a similar street in Sandy Row. Only the neighbours would change, and probably not for the better. There would be a bit of physical space between herself and her parents. The couple had indeed already found a house in Titanic Street which needed a bit of 'doin' up' before they would move in. Until then, they would live with James' parents as James's elder brother had moved out two years previously whilst Shirley still shared a bedroom with her little brother Paul. She looked earnestly at her elder sister: "I'm marrying him for love."

"I know. That's the problem! Ya could have had Stanley Dornan—he was daft about ya an' his da' had several shops on the Newtownards Road."

"Aye, well, it wasn't to be. He was a nice fella but I didn't love him."

"That's not the most important thing! Ya'll see that through time."

"I know what the most important thing for you was—gettin' out of Sandy Row an' movin' up in the world. But look at ya—are ya tryin' to tell me yar happy?"

"No… well, yes an' no… Michael's a nice man an' he's very clean. My ma an' da' like him. Have ya noticed, he's always filin' his fingernails?"

"Aye, he's worse than any girl, I know! My ma calls him a Mary-Jane. But what about… ya know… the other thing?"

"Sex?"

"Aye, sex!"

"We hardly do it. For Michael it's like dippin' into the water at Donaghadee—he's in an' out in two minutes!" The girls burst out laughing. It was still good to share this complicity.

"With James it's very nice!" The younger girl forgot herself.

"Ya mean ya've already done it? Before ya get married? An' yar only eighteen!"

"Almost nineteen, come on! This is the swinging sixties!"

"If my da finds out he'll swing for ya, alright! Although I suppose it's too late now. Where is my da anyway?"

"He went with James an' Paul down to the Ormeau baths for a weddin' scrub. They won't be there again for a long time!" The sisters sat for a moment looking out into the street which was just starting to become very busy as people went to and fro on their weekly shopping errands.

"But yar right, sex is important. It just doesn't have to be with yar husband!"

"Linda! That's shockin'! You better be careful." Shirley suspected that her sister was already unfaithful to her husband. Michael was not quick on the uptake. The women in his life had always ruled the roost and he had made the seamless transition from dominant mother to dominant wife. He surrendered up his pay packet to his wife every week without giving it a second thought.

"I'm careful, don't worry. By the way, James' brother is a nice looker! Another Brylcreem boy!"

"I'm tellin' ya, don't go there!" Linda smiled at her sister but Shirley was no longer smiling. She knew Linda would be influenced by no one as she followed her own appetites through life. She had always been her own mistress.

"He's already married!"

"I'm not lookin' for a husband—remember, I've already got one. Don't be offended, but he is the good-lookin' one of the two." Her sister could be very annoying. The implication was that Linda was also the prettiest of the two sisters, so her and Henry (James' elder brother) were a good match.

Suddenly, their mother's head popped into the parlour:

"You two better get a move on, there's a million things to do before we go to the church. Come on, nigh, stop yar chatterin'!" The girls rose immediately and set about the various tasks before Shirley tried on her wedding dress. They heard her father's voice in the hallway.

"Make sure James isn't with them!" The girl tried to run upstairs in case the groom was also in the hallway but in her hurry, she caught the hem of her long flowing dress with her foot. Her mother was angry when she realised what the tear meant.

"Come on, get that off! I'll sew it… another bloody thing to do!"

"That's a sign of bad luck," said the elder sister.

"Don't say stupid things," retorted the mother, whilst the younger girl looked daggers at her sister as she continued to her bedroom.

Father and young son stepped into the living room—the groom had gone home to dress and make other preparations.

"Did ya have a good scrub?" asked Linda to her young brother.

"I did. It was brilliant—scaldin' hot. My skin's still all wrinkled!"

"You get changed after yar lunch as ya don't want to spill anything on yar good clothes. Don't forget to give yar sister the horseshoe."

"I won't forget, I'm not daft! But I'm starvin' already." The boy went into the scullery to rummage for something to eat but nothing had been left there as the buffet reception would be in a hotel on the Saintfield Road, immediately after the church service. Paul came back into the sitting room saying, "There is no lunch!"

The church service went very well, with Paul presenting his sister with the horseshoe in the grounds of the church, captured by the official photographer. Shirley did drop it getting into the car as she had to be extra careful about the dress but Paul picked it up and gave it to her a second time before everyone bundled into packed cars and drove towards the Ormeau Road.

Everyone was very nervous at the reception. Thank goodness there was an open bar—paid for by the newly-weds who had saved up hard for the big day. Their parents could not afford that extravagant outlay and besides, they knew that no limit would mean that all the guests would be 'plastered' before they even sat down with their food to await the speeches and they did not agree with that.

As expected, by the time the speeches came around, everyone was raucous, falling out of their seats, and unwilling or incapable of listening attentively. No one heard the father's affectionate words and pain at having to 'give away' two daughters in consecutive years—the house would of course be very empty. When he sat down again, the guests were asking each other why he was crying.

The best man had better luck, as everyone was keen on hearing jokes and funny stories about the groom's wayward past. This task fell to his brother Henry who had a stock of stories to tell from their shared childhood and adolescent experiences. He ran through these with great gusto, speaking softly only when it came to the lewd bits everyone was waiting for. From time to time, his eyes would meet those of

Linda, who was very discreet because of the presence of her husband, but also very encouraging. Shirley was not happy with the exchanges for she knew they would soon be lovers. She felt worried about her sister.

The speeches were followed by dessert and then more insatiable drinking and riotous dancing until Henry's wife went home because of the unbearable noise which had given her a headache. He had anticipated this and in fact, had been looking forward to it.

Tables began breaking up and reforming, although James stayed with his brother and the two sisters. Michael had gone over to keep his parents-in-law company. When the lights dimmed and the music slowed, Henry went over to ask Michael if he could ask his wife up for a dance. Permission was of course granted. It was a respectable event at the beginning, both parties keeping a guarded distance until they were away from certain lines of vision, and then Henry ran his fingers playfully down his sister-in-law's back.

Shirley went to talk to Michael and shield him from any improper view. When the music was over, she went back to James who was downing the last of his pint.

"I don't like it. Ya know what they're up to." This was not a question; both were very aware of what was going on but had different perspectives on the subject: James had a certain admiration for his brother whilst Shirley disapproved and was frightened by, her sister's libertine behaviour. She was fearful of the future consequences. And the possible embarrassment! Besides, she felt sorry for Michael and made her opinion clear to her husband.

"Don't waste yar time feelin' sorry for that dopey gat! On top o' everything, he's such an oul' Jinny-Anne… ya go out for a pint o' Guinness wi' him and he orders a half o' lager. Once he drinks almost two-thirds of it, he leaves ya sittin' on yar own t' go an' visit his ma. He's hardly what you'd call a man's man."

"That's the way my sister picks them! There's the man ya marry an' the man ya'd never want to marry 'cause ya know he would never be faithful."

"So, I'm the type a girl should marry? A safe bet?"

"That's not why I chose you an' you know that." James shook his head approvingly.

After two weeks spent in a cheap guesthouse in Portrush for their honeymoon, the couple returned to Belfast and began a new life in their home in Titanic Street which Shirley's father had made liveable, with wallpaper and paint, during their absence. He also managed to furnish it partially with decent second-hand purchases which the couple would add to when they had earned enough money. For the present, it was enough to start up with and they were both grateful to him.

The Saturday morning after their return, Shirley received the visit of her sister. They were both glad to see each other. Shirley put the kettle on whilst her sister put some buns she had just bought, on a plate and sat down at the slightly-scored drop-leaf table. She scrutinised the second-hand furniture disapprovingly and then said out loud: "My da did well for yous!"

"Aye, he did," said Shirley, bringing in the tea.

"I'm changing my settee and chairs and thought they might look alright here—if ya fancy them."

"Aye, I do… that would be great! Thanks very much, my arse is already killin' me on these wooden seats!"

"When Gilpins deliver to me, I'll get them to drop off the old suite to you. Not that it's very old, as ya know. Hardly a year."

"Sure, it'll be dead on." Shirley did not want to ask why her sister was already changing her settee and armchairs as she feared the answer might contain a veiled insult to her own expectations in life.

There was a lull in the conversation while they drank tea and cautiously ate a jam doughnut. Then Linda asked where 'the hubby' was.

"He's away to see someone about a motorbike. He'll need some form of transport to get to his work from here." Her sister nodded in agreement. Shirley looked her fixedly in the eyes and asked what she had been dying to ask:

"Did anything happen between you an' Henry—yous looked to be getting very close to each other."

"It did. In fact, the first Saturday yous were away he took me to the Glens of Antrim in his car. We enjoyed it!"

"I'm sure yous did!"

"We even mentioned drivin' down to Portrush to make it a foursome for the day." Shirley knew her sister was just being provocative.

"Well, I'm glad ya didn't do that."

"Do I sense you don't approve? You just wait until you've been married for a bit, ya'll see."

"I don't think so. When are you seein' him again?"

"I'm not. It's over. It was just a bit o' fun. Besides that, I've met a soldier stationed down in Antrim—nigh he's a lot o' fun!"

When her sister had left the house to visit their mother, Shirley sat both relieved and worried. She was indeed thankful for the fact that no one had found out about Linda's 'fling'. What she had gleaned from her sister's extra-marital experiences and her husband's recent remarks, offered her little reassurance as regards her own marriage or the future tensions which she already sensed to be gathering on the horizon. "A marriage is what you make it," is what she had often heard her mother say. Shirley wondered how many unexplained absences and unresolved questions her mother had had to come to terms with. She thought about her sister again and remembered reading, in one of her magazines, the saying: 'What the eye does not see, the heart does not grieve over.' She felt that she had not really understood it and even questioned why anyone would write it. To Shirley, it was totally unsatisfactory, as if someone was just happy to sidestep an important issue. Now, as she stared into her empty teacup, she felt even more perplexed.

The Sorter

John Spence lived in number 35 Kensington Street and everyday dreamed of winning money. He was convinced that he was a naturally unlucky person, having four daughters and no sons, but this conviction did not stop him from indulging in various forms of gambling every week in life—from 'the Pools' and Spot the Ball to a Saturday flutter on the 'gee-gees.' When possible, he would play the dates of birth of his four girls—some combination of the day, the month or the year. They were the living symbols of his bad luck in life but perhaps, by their very irrefutable existence, they might be able to reverse the trend. At least, that was the motivation he clung to each week on setting out to spend Saturday morning in the bookies almost opposite his house.

Since the birth of his second daughter, John had come to secretly resent his wife. The resentment increased with the birth of each girl until he was fully persuaded that his wife was stricken by some sort of curse. When he had a few drinks on a Friday night, this curse became tangible to him and his wife had consequently learned to keep a low profile at the weekend.

John and his wife slept in the front bedroom whilst the girls slept in the back room which gave on to the yard and the row of houses behind. They enjoyed talking and laughing until late at night but when they heard their father return from Mosie Hunter's pub on a Friday evening, they would respect total silence until his heavy snoring told them the household was safe until the morrow.

It happened that one Friday in May, John had come home from his work in the General Post Office in Royal Avenue, Belfast; had his dinner; changed his shirt and gone out to the pub for the evening. In their father's absence, a good-humoured and carefree atmosphere reigned in the household and this lasted until the man of the house was heard to stagger through the front door and then make his way clumsily and noisily up the stairs to his bedroom. The girls listened attentively to his undressing. That is when his voice angrily broke the silence:

"That bastard McGivern has had another son!" His speech was slow and deliberate with a marked slur. The girls battened down for the night—there would be no more chatter from them. They heard their father rant on until he became completely unintelligible, but no sound was heard from their mother. She was wisely pretending to be asleep.

John awoke early next morning with a splitting headache and an inability to move from the bed. He stretched out his arm slowly to feel if his wife was beside him: she was not. He was both relieved and disappointed by her absence. He soon remembered why he resented her and his anger began to form again under the pressure of his hangover. He heard her come gingerly up the stairs and on opening the door she greeted him with, "I've brought ya a nice cup o' tea seein' as ya might be feelin' a bit out o' sorts, ya know?"

"Ya can keep yar bloody tea, Woman!" John's anger had gathered to a point of rupture which his wife immediately recognised and which convinced her that it would be best to beat a silently strategic retreat.

"Where d'ya think yar goin'?" John sprung out of bed and grabbed his wife before she could completely leave the room. She was startled by his newly found agility and the energetic lunge with which he grabbed her by both arms, steadying himself at the same time. He looked at her with bloodshot eyes full of malicious intent.

"Yar hurtin' me!" His wife did not shout in spite of the pain of his powerful grip as she did not want her girls to be frightened.

John had never hurt her before. It happened on one occasion that, in order not to hurt his wife—whom he thought had pushed him beyond the pale with her cutting retorts—John had struck the wall mirror with his fist and had to be taken to the Royal Hospital to have several stitches inserted. His reflex was similar on this occasion and on hearing her complaint, he turned sharply and kicked the foot of their iron bedstead. He was of course barefoot and the result was instantaneous. John almost jumped into the air because of the excruciating pain which shot through his big toe and shook his entire being until he fell over on to the bed. His wife did not know what to do.

"Ack, John what've ya done ta yarself?" John half-tried to kick her away with his other foot but she was skilful enough to remain just out of his range.

Fridges in the sixties were not common in Kensington Street but it was a sign of their improving conditions that the Spences had managed to purchase one 'on tick' from Gilpins furniture shop in Sandy Row. The weekly financial contribution from the eldest girl, who had started a job in the Linfield Mill, was essential to this purchase, so at least there was something positive to be gained from the girls' participation in household matters – until they got married, of course. John's wife hurried downstairs and soon came up with a basin of water with ice bobbing on the surface.

"Here, put yar foot into this… it will stop the swellin'."

John knew this was the action to be taken and he quickly lowered his foot into the water. His big toe was already very swollen and bent, so that the articulation looked permanently hooked.

"I think that might be broken." She said concernedly. "Ya'll have to go to the hospital."

John looked at her venomously.

"I'm not goin' to any friggin' hospital, Woman!" She knew it would be useless to argue, so she went downstairs again to fetch tablets and a glass of water for her husband. She told the girls their father had hurt himself and that they had to be quiet. There was a list with some money on the mantlepiece so they could do the shopping for once.

She gave her husband two painkillers and suggested that he lie on the bed. She dried his foot very carefully and swung his leg slowly on to the bed.

"I'll break more ice and make ya a wee compress." Despite his paralysing pain, John looked up at his wife where he saw the genuine concern for him in her eyes. He managed to mutter a begrudged 'thanks'.

The pain in his foot was so intense that it made him unaware of his headache and other nauseating effects of his hangover. It turned his anger to self-pity as he realised, he would not be able to walk to the bookmakers this morning nor do any of the things that made his weekend especially relaxing. He would have to confine himself to the bedroom and bear the stupidity and frustration of his self-inflicted agony.

John spent hours lying in bed until the pain slightly subsided and he was able to consider all the implications of his injury. From the nebulosity of his still intoxicated brain came a plan. At first, it was just an idea which grew into a strong desire that soon took the form of a strategy. He had it! He had formulated a battle plan!

No, he would definitely not go to the hospital. In fact, no one else must know that he had hurt his foot and that the toe was almost certainly broken. He would remain in bed all weekend and then on Monday morning he would get his brother-in-law to drive him to work where he would show up and walk about as if nothing had happened. He knew this would take an almighty effort because the pain would still be intense, but he felt that he was up to the task and the end result would be worth all the suffering. He would then take the first opportunity to go into the storeroom where he went every morning to get his baskets of mail to sort. There were other boxes, heavy ones, which sat on the storage racks until moved elsewhere and he would choose one of the heaviest to perform the operation. He would select the appropriate box and, with no one around, would drop it on his foot and lie screaming until someone came to help him. This was the plan! He knew it would work—knew that at the very least it would get him a job sitting at a desk rather than standing all day, endlessly sorting letters and parcels. He believed also that the General Post Office would settle up with him without going to court or a tribunal and that he would consequently come into a very healthy sum of money.

With these thoughts, John was able to smile through his pain and eventually fall into a deep sleep.

He was awakened just before one o'clock by his wife who shuffled her way cautiously through the bedroom door carrying scrambled eggs, toast and tea on a tray which she put on the bedside table.

"I was up earlier but ya were sleepin' so I just let ya sleep. Best thing for 'im, I says to meself." She placed extra pillows behind her husband's back to get him into an almost seated position. "Are ya sure ya don't want to go to the hospital, John?"

John groaned and screwed up his face as he took his wife's hand. She wondered what he was going to do now and tried to hold herself aloof but the mildness of his voice surprised her and indicated that he meant no harm towards her.

"Listen, Ginny," John rarely called her by her first name so she decided that what he had to say must be of the utmost importance. She sat her thin frame down delicately on the edge of the bed.

"Ginny… I have a plan… I've already given it a lot o' thought. I'm not goin' to the hospital. On Monday ya'll have to ask yar brother to take me to work. I'm goin' to pretend there's nothin' wrong wi' me an' then I'm goin' to drop a box on my foot an' put in a claim with the post office." His wife was so taken aback that she could not utter a word. John went on:

"Tomorrow ya'll have to help me practice walkin' about the bedroom. I won't be able to wear shoes but I can wear my sandals and a pair o' socks, okay?"

Ginny nodded. "Do ya think it will work, John?" she asked innocently.

"Aye, certainly it'll work! Ya'll see, we'll soon be movin' outta this dump of a house." John smiled at his wife. She felt happy as they now had a project to be working on together. It would be the best thing that could happen to the girls and good for the atmosphere in their home.

"And make sure ya don't tell anybody—make sure the girls don't say I hurt ma foot to anybody even their uncle."

"Ya better ate yar eggs and keep yar strength up!" Ginny squeezed her husband's hand and then rose to her feet to leave the bedroom.

The rest of the weekend was spent working out every detail of the plan. Ginny cautioned the girls and concocted a story for her brother about her husband not feeling well but having to go to work nonetheless as he had an interview with his boss concerning promotion. She visited the brother on Sunday evening to make her request which was immediately granted. Her brother was retired and only too happy to see that the ne'er-do-well John might at last be coming up in the world.

On Monday morning, John was driven to work as planned. The weather was clement and no one would remark upon the sandals, as long as they did not look too long at the right foot which had a noticeably swollen big toe which was only partially concealed by the specially chosen black socks. John got out of the car smiling and suppressing the pain he was acutely experiencing. He waved his brother-in-law off.

He carried out his plan to the last detail—beginning by smiling profusely with his pleasant 'Good mornings!' to everyone, down to the moment when, hearing his cry, a colleague ran in to help John who was lying prostrate on the floor beside a very heavy package containing metallic parts for the various racks that were still to go up. John's pain was of course very real: he had selected and dropped the package directly on his right foot, the result being that it took him a couple of minutes to overcome the agony in order to externalise his pain into a dreadful howl for help. He was taken to the Royal Victoria Hospital where he was indeed diagnosed with a broken toe as well as a badly crushed foot.

It was several weeks before John Spence returned to his work in Royal Avenue, albeit with a walking stick. As anticipated, he was immediately given a job behind the counter where he could deal directly with the public, thus becoming the amiable and welcoming face of the GPO to thousands of people. He was excellent at his job, so much so that his boss asked himself why he had not put honest John there ages ago. He obviously knew how to deal with difficult customers and was undoubtedly a considerable asset to their important institution.

Of course, John put in a claim for compensation for his accident—he was even encouraged to do so by his boss. After about eighteen months, he received a cheque for the sum of thirty-five thousand pounds which, in his wisdom, he decided not to contest.

The family moved to a much larger house in Donegall Avenue where his girls were only two per bedroom and where he had an inside toilet and hot running water. He never went to the bookmakers again but joined a syndicate to do the Pools each week, always playing the same dates of birth. He included his wife's date in this as he now looked upon her as being partly responsible for his good fortune. Her role was of course minor when compared to his own expertly masterminded scheme which he looked back on with a certain degree of smugness.

The Tin Pot Man

Derek lived in Stroud Street, almost opposite Minnie Mack, who I was obliged to visit once a week with my mother as Minnie did not get out much because of her weight and hardly ever went to do 'the messages' in Sandy Row. My mum always got a few things in for her on a Saturday even though she did have a fairly sprightly husband, Eddie—but who was not one for shopping.

Approaching Minnie's house, I would always look across the street at Derek's shabby front door in case he would emerge, but he never did. His downstairs window was filthy but I would often press my forehead against it on the way to school and could just distinguish a dingy, brownish screen which cut the rest of the small room off from view. Along with the filth, it was a second strategic barrier which shielded Derek from the outside world. No one I knew—not even close neighbours—had ever been inside the house.

It was not wise to be a loner in our community. Derek was obviously a bit 'cracked', which meant that adults would keep their distance and children would victimise him whenever the opportunity arose. Halloween was the perfect opportunity as fireworks could be thrown through his letterbox, but bangers were also frequent any weekend when the weather allowed kids out until after dark.

Derek would often be tempted out by the good weather. He would take a chair, walk to the top of Combermere Street, then sit for hours watching the cars and buses go by on the Donegall Road. As he sat perched on his chair, Derek always wore a tin pot on his head and frequently held a handkerchief soaked in vinegar to his mouth and nose. This did not stop a continuous flow of verbal abuse from him which was not directed at anyone in particular. Nevertheless, churchgoers were offended and young couples crossed the road to get out of earshot. Local men sometimes tried to enter into conversation with him but to no avail. You could hear the odd 'Oright Deek?' as someone sauntered past him on their way to the Clock Bar but this was met with no recognition.

The tin pot was slightly bowl-shaped and had a rim which made it look vaguely like an antiquated British war helmet and Derek used it to boil water on a camping stove, for it was blackened on the top. From a particular angle, it also resembled one of those bowler-hats the Orangemen parade in during the July marches. As I was growing up, I had several theories about these idiosyncrasies of his. At one point, I was convinced that he wore the tin pot so that if we were under surveillance by extra-terrestrial creatures, the latter would not be able to read his thoughts. I once developed a theory about the handkerchief which I imagined Derek used to stop his soul escaping from his body. I read somewhere that certain religious people believed this possible. But none of my explanations seemed to be appropriate when applied to Derek.

To the younger boys in the streets around, Derek was a bit of a bogeyman and they attempted no approach to him that had any friendliness attached to it. He was frequently taunted—from a safe distance, because the man, in his sixties now, was light and nimble and quick to react to any screams or offensive yells. Fortunately, he could no longer run fast enough to catch any of us but the threat was forever present. I always observed his spasmodic movements closely and kept a sharp eye on his house when going to Minnie Mack's in case he recognised me as one of those who threw bangers through his letterbox. I was one of his childhood persecutors.

I remember one early summer evening in June after tea when I walked past Derek—on the other side of the road of course and observed him rocking to and fro as if he was chanting something. He did not look at me. I was curious to know what he was saying so I walked around the block and came up behind him from Stroud Street. I was very careful not to make a sound but as I approached, he stopped suddenly and listened. I froze and he went back to his monologue punctuated with obscenities. He was talking to himself, making statements, asking and giving answers that seemed to be nonsense.

I caught words at random: "Fuckin' bastards smashed Albert… Aye, did a good fuckin' job, didn't they? Aye, they did indeed, cunts!"

I was wondering to myself who he was talking about—there was a married man called Albert who lived on our street but I was not aware anything bad had happened to him—when a middle-aged neighbour approached on his way to the Clock. Men often put time in the Clock rather than go to Mosie Hunter's or the Albion Bar—which were at opposing ends of Kensington Street—when they wanted a more discreet drink. He looked at the seated figure clutching the hanky to his face and said "What about ya, Deek?" He seemed to hope for an answer but only got a few more obscene and unintelligible words about Albert.

"Give my best to Albert, Deek!" and he was about to move on when he glanced at me. He said nothing, but his look implied that I should be careful and back off. I did exactly that and then went home, leaving Derek to his enigmatic worlds.

I cannot say that I developed any sympathy for the man or even empathy for his loner status in the community, but I did feel less frightened of him. And in spite of being drawn to know more about the solitary figure, I remained part of his persecution squad. On the following eleventh night, 1 still jammed fireworks through his letterbox and laughed with the others as he ran out of the house effing and blinding, and continue until he realised that he had forgotten his tin pot and so run back inside.

Later in August, when I was returning from flirting with a girl I had attended Blythe Street primary school with, I was walking slowly past Derek's house when I saw a dim light quiver through the almost blacked-out interior. There was an almighty raucous uproar going on and it sounded like Derek was having a fierce argument with some unwelcome presence. The evening was getting dark so I moved to the door and began listening in relative safety, pushing up the swinging rectangular flap in order to hear better.

Derek's voice rose accusingly: "You… you… you were the fuckin' bastard… ya gat 's all shot to pieces, you were the fuckin' enemy, ya cunt… shoulda blown yar fuckin' head off when a had a chance." A short silence was then followed by a muffled smash into what sounded like a table. Then came muted sobs, broken by parts of words which made no sense except that I was able to understand from piecing them together that Albert was not a person but a place. I could not bear to listen to any more of Derek's rage, sufferings and lamentations, so I walked quietly home.

Like many children in Sandy Row, I grew up in a home without books, so on Saturday mornings I started going to the local library on the Donegall Road to borrow books that were on my A-Level programme. I managed to stretch the term 'borrow' to make some of these into very long-term loans. I had thought about Derek's words and on the Saturday following my indiscretion, I decided to ask the librarian if he knew where Albert was. He also understood that Albert was a person and looked at me quizzically.

I explained and he then said: "You're talking about the town in France—the main regrouping town for troops during the Battle of the Somme. A lot of our boys died around there."

I had heard about the Somme—had seen it written on flags and banners the Orangemen poudly hold during the Twelfth marches but the word did not mean anything to me. When the librarian asked what the origin of my question was, I told him about Derek's rantings. He had heard of Derek.

"Sometimes sits at the top of the street with a tin pot on his head! Aye, Derek Colquhoun… fought at the Battle of the Somme. I never knew him… different generation… but my father told me about him. Terrible shame to see him today. Lost his marlies, I'm afraid. Many of those who came back were never the same. But we have a few books on the Somme if you want to take one out."

I took out the first book I found on the shelf he pointed out to me but when I got it home, I found that it was mainly about life in the trenches. The most impressive thing for me was the way the soldiers looked challengingly into the camera. They made me feel uncomfortable, somehow guilty.

I saw Derek only once more: it was in September 1971 when I accompanied my father on vigilante duty—it was just getting dark and we were on our way back home from Sandy Row to Shaftesbury Square. After walking past him, I decided to double back and make my way quietly up behind him. I thought that I understood him more and that this was my chance to befriend him. He was probably the only real 'hero' I would ever meet. After warning me to be careful and not approach too closely, my father walked on, looking back from time to time.

The strange thing on this occasion was that Derek was silent. He was wearing his tin hat and holding his dripping hankie, but his head was slumped slightly forward and his eyes were closed. I moved around his chair and he seemed to be unaware of my presence. Finally, I stood in front of him and said quietly: "I saw pictures of the Thiepval Tower."

On hearing the word 'Thiepval', his head shot up and his eyes opened wide. He stared at me fixedly as if he had seen a ghost. I did not know what to say or do so I apologised for having startled him. He began ranting again in his most obscene manner and became increasingly more agitated. I felt it was time to back off and leave him alone.

I looked at him once more, straight into those dark, deep, unfathomable eyes, and bid him a pleasant 'Goodnight'. I received the only response I have ever heard him make directly to another human being:

"Ya wee fuckin' eejit!"

I caught up with my father at the top of Kensington Street where he was waiting for me. He saw that I was a bit shaken.

"Not a great one for conversation, eh son?"

"That's true… he's a hard man to get to know." My father smiled at me as we walked down the street.

I did check on Derek once or twice before leaving Belfast the following July. I tried peering through the window and listening in at the door but I saw and heard nothing. I went past the top of Combermere Street on many occasions during that final year but I never saw Derek again. I think it is safe to say that, mysteriously, he disappeared with the 'Troubles'.

The Doll

Helen Morrow was thirteen, one year older than Martin Scott, when the pair sat in the June sunshine on the kerb close to her house in Wesley Street. They talked mainly about the summer holidays. Helen was going with her elder sister to spend a week in her aunt's caravan in Millisle whilst Martin would be leaving Northern Ireland for the first time as his newly-wed sister, Trudy, had booked for two weeks on the Isle of Man during the July fortnight and had promised to take him with the couple. Trudy took her younger brother everywhere with her. Martin was very excited about the trip.

"I'll bring ya back a present from Millisle," said Helen, looking teasingly into Martin's wide-green eyes.

"Will ya? I'll bring you one too from the Isle of Man."

There was almost an immediate feeling of regret at this promise, as Martin realised he would have very little money, and a present for a thirteen-year old girl would be hard to come by. At this point, he could not even imagine what such a present could be. He would probably have to ask his sister, although that thought made him feel uneasy as she probably would not approve. His uneasiness was soon dispelled though by Helen discreetly taking his hand. He looked around to see if anyone was watching them. The youngsters had already kissed but this was neither the time nor the place for any more daring demonstration of sexual interest. They sat quietly under the warmth of the afternoon sun until a voice came from the hallway behind them.

"Helen, I need yar help with the ironin'." It was her elder sister's voice which severed their handholding. They both slowly stood up.

"Will I see ya tamara?" the girl asked innocently.

"I don't know. I'll have to go to church and then help ma mammy. My daddy's still away." Martin's father was in the RAF and spent much of the week touring around the province on a recruitment drive. Along with another corporal, he slept in a caravan if they were too far from Belfast. At present they were in Enniskillen.

"Sure, if I don't see ya, I'll see ya durin' the week, after school." This was agreed upon and the lad and girl reluctantly left one another and went their separate ways.

Since her recent marriage, the only opportunity Martin had to talk with his sister was on a Saturday morning when both his sisters would call in to see their mother for a weekly chat. Trudy arrived at about ten o'clock and after a friendly 'Hi ya!', she went straight into the kitchen to talk with her mother. Martin sat on the stairs, watching them drinking tea at the folding table and chatting lively. They seemed to talk forever and Martin was about to abandon his idea concerning the present when his sister stood up and said 'Cheerio' to her mother. She looked at him as she walked through the tiny, over-furnished sitting-room.

"Have you bin sittin' there all this time?"

"Not much else to do this mornin'." His sister was about to leave the house when he added: "I wanted to ask ya something…"

"Go ahead."

"I was thinkin' of bringin' a present back for someone from the Isle of Man… do ya think it will be very dear? For a girl."

"Is that for Helen Morrow?" His sister had seen them walking around the streets together. And he was right—she did not approve.

"Let me tell ya something… if she's anything like her big sister she won't bring ya a present." Trudy had gone to school with Helen's elder sister and did not at all appreciate the girl.

"She will. She told me she would bring me a present from Millisle."

"Listen Son, you spend your money on yourself—you won't have that much. An' ya can bring back a wee glass animal for yer mammy—I know they do a lot o' those over there."

Martin did not appear convinced that this was the appropriate solution to his dilemma, so his sister moved closer to him and stroked his cheek.

"Mind my words: she won't bring you any present."

With this warning, she left the house and stepped into the street at the same time as their elder sister arrived to see her mother. Martin went up to his bedroom.

The lad saw his girlfriend several times a week before leaving for the Isle of Man during the annual July fortnight break. Talk of a present came up once or twice and Martin felt certain that Helen would definitely bring him back something. She gave him to understand that she knew what his present would be but this caused him to be more stressed as he had no idea what he could give her. In fact, he had no idea what would be suitable and if his sister did not provide him with any suggestions—which she did not seem inclined to do—then he would probably come back with nothing. It was a miserable state of affairs.

The sea crossing from Belfast to Douglas proved to be very rough. Despite taking a sea-sick tablet, the boy was ill several times and only picked up when he set foot on solid ground. Fortunately, they were only a short bus ride to the caravan park where they would spend the next two weeks overlooking the sea. His sister remarked enthusiastically that the weather was turning out good too and was supposed to stay that way for at least a few days. Martin relaxed at last—he had arrived in paradise.

The two weeks on the Isle of Man were spent in bus rides in and out of town; walking along the promenade; going to amusement halls and taking photos. There were several places along the seafront organising photo-shots with huge cut-outs of beach scenes, displaying muscular men and curvy ladies. Martin had to smile and put his head through several of these holes to show they were all having a good time, with one special photo for his parents where he was pictured pretending to drink from a plastic pint of Guinness which was half his size. It seemed to amuse his sister.

Money was of course a concern. He arrived with two half-crowns and was very careful not to spend much on ice-cream and candy floss, despite his sister's encouragement. They did find a glassblower in the town where he purchased a small, colourful, but very fragile deer for his mother which cost him a shilling. He was happy getting to the end of his stay with more than three shillings left but he still had no inkling as to what he could buy Helen. Besides, he was constantly aware that his sister was watching him closely every time he would stop to look at some article of leather or jewellery suitable for a teenage girl. In the end, he abandoned the idea of a present and decided to take his remaining money home with him in order to buy something in a local shop, even if it meant pretending about the origin of the article. He had approximately one week to find something suitable as Helen's holiday in Millisle began on the day of his return to Belfast. But he was conscious that the decision was more a way of postponing his stay of execution.

A lucky thing happened to Martin on the Monday following his return: one of his mother's club friends from the Shankill came round to talk about events that they were planning for the coming year. Martin was trying to watch TV as they chatted noisily together but at one point, he distinctly heard the woman say that she had sold quite a few dolls over the summer. Apparently, she made them herself. His mother had already seen one or two and was full of praise—especially for the added income they brought. When the woman was about to set off for home, Martin left them and waited outside in the street where it was now getting dark. When she came out and started walking to the bus stop, he ran after her: "Excuse me, did I hear you say you made dolls?" She nodded at him, smiling broadly.

"How much are they?"

"Four shillings." Martin became despondent and looked at the pavement.

"Why?"

" 'cause I've only gat about three shillings left from my holidays."

The woman said that she would do it for three shillings—it would just about cover the materials. She asked him the colour of the dress and when he said 'blue' she nodded approvingly and promised to do it for the following Friday. Martin was very happy but asked the woman not to tell anyone as it was to be a surprise. She agreed and rushed off to get her bus.

When the doll duly arrived on the Friday afternoon, Martin took the large paper bag upstairs and left his mother and her friend downstairs to chat over a cup of tea. His mother was now aware of the purchase but he knew she would not say anything. He sat on his bed and pulled the doll from its outer envelope, gingerly undoing the tissue paper around it. It did look quite splendid: the blue dress puffed out from the waist down and was covered with sequins and gold braid. He lifted the dress up to look underneath and saw that the doll was not wearing knickers, which surprised him. Perhaps she had economised on the underwear. The dress was of the same colour as the eyes which were a deep blue framed by long-dark eyelashes and when he tilted it on its back, the eyes automatically closed. The face and body were of a hard plastic and when he tapped the head it sounded hollow. But he was more than happy with the result. He would hide it in his room until the next day.

Helen would be back on Saturday morning and Martin calculated that his best chance to see the girl would be just before lunch. He sat in his room making his preparations whilst listening to the voices of his two sisters and mother downstairs. Unfortunately for Martin, the sisters would be staying for lunch: there was not much chance of getting out of the house without being seen. Martin would have to steel himself against any embarrassing remarks. He went quietly downstairs, holding the present in his right hand in order to try to hide it from view. He said 'Hello', but both sisters had their eyes on the object in his right hand.

Once outside, Martin moved quickly. He was happy with his gift. He reached Helen's house and knocked on the door. Helen was all smiles when she greeted him.

"I don't have much time as I have to help my sister."

"That's okay. I just came round to give you this." Martin held out his gift to the still smiling girl. She eagerly unwrapped it and held it up to the light like a trophy.

"It's lovely! Thank you very much!" Martin waited expectantly until the girl said: "I haven't got a present for you, I'm sorry. I did have one but I left it on the train. I'm really sorry!"

"That's alright." Martin tried to conceal his disappointment. He turned away and quietly said: "See ya." The girl replied the same and closed the hall door.

His sister was right! She was right! Why hadn't he listened?

When he arrived home, seeing the sorrow in his eyes, the sisters remained quiet. They knew their brother had received nothing from the girl. Martin finally broke the silence: "She forgot my present on the train."

The sisters still said nothing. Martin went upstairs to his room to lie on his bed. It occurred to him that he should have asked Helen what his present was supposed to have been. But then he was glad he had not. After all, it was now of no importance. Better to forget about the whole episode.

Approximately ten minutes passed when he heard someone on the stairs. His sister knocked on his door and when he opened it, she handed him the doll.

"I went an' got it back for ya. I told her big sister I'd bust her gob if she didn't get it back… an' she knew I was serious!" Martin took the doll and looked at it incredulously—his sister had actually gone around to their house and threatened them! He looked at her in admiration and they exchanged smiles of recognition.

When alone, Martin wondered what he was going to do with the doll. Perhaps keep it for someone else. He was tempted to throw it in the bin. He gazed into its deep-blue eyes and then tilted it backwards to see them slowly close.

"She could have put knickers on it!" he said to himself.

The Books

Paul came out of his bedroom at about half-past nine on the Sunday morning. He looked through his parents' open bedroom door and saw that the room was empty. He listened closely until he could distinguish his father's slow and deliberate movements as he went about dealing with pots and dishes in the kitchen which had remained there unwashed from the night before. He could smell the smoke of a cigarette which meant that his mother was probably sitting in her armchair with her morning cup of tea. She never ate breakfast. Paul looked at what he recognised as a magazine on the floor beside the bed—it had probably slipped out of the sleeping reader's hands and dropped on the floor. It was certainly some sort of crime magazine—*True Detective* or something of that nature. The boy walked into the other bedroom and picked up the magazine. He began reading to himself:

Detectives John Kruger and William Hardy paced around the neat and tidy apartment looking for other indications of the murderer's visit. They found nothing of interest. The crime would be another hard nut to crack. John went back into the living-room where the wife was sprawled on the carpet beside the coffee-table. She had been shot three times in the stomach and chest and had bled profusely before leaving this world. At least she had a quiet and relatively quick death. John Kruger followed the trail of blood left by her husband. He had been less fortunate. The assailant had beaten him savagely several times over the head with some sort of metallic cosh that was no longer visible on the scene of the crime. Part of the back of the skull had caved in, revealing an amass of blood, flesh, and bone. Still, the husband had managed to crawl into the kitchen where he was stabbed several times with a carving knife which now lay in the pool of blood beside him. John would wait on the arrival of Forensics before turning him over. He wanted to avoid more blood on his shoes and certainly not get any on the two-hundred-dollar suit that his wife had just purchased for his promotion party. He looked at the blood as if it contained some sort of hidden message.

Bill Hardy came back into the room.

"Guess this will be another one we'll put down to the New Jersey serial killer."

John nodded to his partner saying: "But we know the assailant knew his victims. This was no ordinary killing."

More sirens could be heard blaring down the street as Forensics started to arrive.

Paul turned back to the cover page which was filled with pictures of terrified and screaming women, threatening male shadows with guns, and headlines about sadistic campus killers and men hallucinating about Jesus. 'Riveting stuff!' he said to himself. He smilingly shook his head and placed the magazine in its position on the floor before leaving the room to go quietly downstairs. As anticipated, he found his mother smoking and drinking tea in her armchair before the coal fire.

"Did ya sleep alright, Son?"

"I did thanks." Paul stood for a moment looking into the red coals.

"Yer da's makin' a bit o' breakfast—away in an' tell 'im what ya want."

Once in the kitchen, the father looked at his son: "I'm fryin' up—d'ya want some bacon, eggs an' beans… or mushrooms an' sausages… or fried bread…" The father inevitably went through a list of things people could have to eat. He was always happy to offer an abundance. The boy just fancied tea and toast.

"Not worth botherin' about… tea an' toast! Go an' sit wi' yar ma an' I'll bring it in to ya."

"Da, I wanted to ask ya something: tell us this, why d'ya read all those crime and true detective magazines? I never see ya readin' anything else." The son did not think there was anything sinister in this choice of literature but he was just curious.

"I don't know son. I can't say I read them because it takes me a week to get beyond the first page. I read a paragraph and then fall asleep an' the next night I read the same paragraph again—sometimes I get a few more sentences read before fallin' asleep! I'm not a reader. I've never read a whole book in ma life." The boy was not sure if his father was proud of the last statement but he knew that he was perfectly honest about the function and manner of his father's reading.

"Nigh, yar ma there… she's a reader! She loves those magazines and she gets through so many crime books as well. She loves a good murder story!"

Paul knew that this too was true. His mother also loved horror films.

Paul walked into the sitting-room and began to put his shoes on. He was sixteen now and no longer went to church on a Sunday.

"I'll just go an' get the paper from Harry Robinson. Be back in a minute." He took some money from the mantlepiece.

"Get me a paper too!" It had become a custom for him to buy two Sunday papers—*The News of the World* for his parents and *The Sunday Times* for himself. He would sit and read for hours on a Sunday and his father would always make the same remark: "I don't see how ya can read all that in one day. It's beyond me!"

The boy got back in time for the arrival of his tea and toast.

Paul had grown up in a house where, apart from crime fiction, there were absolutely no books. There was nothing exceptional about this—there were no books in any of his friends' houses either. But he had just finished his O-levels and was embarked now on his A-levels and he was starting to feel the need for 'real' books: to be able to leaf through a book that would give you some vital information about life, or at least access to another universe, even if 'unreal'. This is when, like the other scattering of adolescents in the area who were fortunate to continue their education beyond the age of fifteen, he started to frequent the Donegall Road Library, which was only about ten or fifteen minutes from his home.

The texts on his A-level literature programme were of course provided by his grammar school, so it was mainly texts of criticism that he set out to borrow from the local library. He entered the very warm and partly sunlit library on a

Saturday morning in September 1970, looking for books on Milton, T.S. Eliot and D.H. Lawrence in particular. He immediately took in the smell of the place: it was fusty but warm and reassuring, with an odour of matured wood mixed with wax and pipe tobacco. There was wood everywhere: it encased the books and composed the surrounding chairs, tables and wall panels. He went straight to the front desk and proudly registered to be a member of this new fraternity.

He had a curious feeling of being at home as he placed his backpack on one of the tables set aside for individual work and began looking for the literature section which he soon came across. There were numerous books available for his purposes and he skimmed through several with a great sense of pleasure and belonging. He knew this place was where he should be, or at least, where he wanted to be.

Paul selected half a dozen books and took them to his secluded desk. He would be allowed to take home three but after narrowing down his selection, he still found himself with four books. He looked over at the front desk, watching people bring their books to be stamped and then leaving nonchalantly through the heavy doors of the main entrance. He would do the same but before that he would slip the smallest volume into his backpack. He discreetly looked around him before carrying out this task, put the other two books back on the shelf and then made his way to the front desk where a young lady took out his newly prepared card which she stamped before stamping the books in his hand with the date they were due back on. Paul smiled and exited the building.

As he walked down the Donegall Road he told himself that he was only borrowing the book—a long-term loan. It was not stealing. This is how he justified the 'borrowing' of books over the next two years. He did not take one per week but by the end of June 1972, he had thirty-eight volumes of varied literary criticism on his bedroom bookshelves, all stamped in several places throughout with 'Belfast Donegall Road Library'. His parents were never suspicious of the origin of the books. In fact, they were not interested enough to even open one of them. His father simply remarked on several occasions that he did not understand how anyone could read so many books and even jokingly doubted that he was the legitimate progenitor of this avid reader. The secret role of the milkman, postman, or some alien creature, was often evoked on these occasions.

Paul successfully passed his A-levels and obtained a university place in England. He was eager to get away from 'troubled' Belfast. His parents too, had just been waiting for him to finish his exams to move to Lancashire where they had relatives who could put them up until they were allocated a council house. As everyone began the packing up, Paul looked as his 'borrowed' library books. The subject had finally come to its closure. He would of course return them but would have to concoct some sort of story to have them accepted into the library once more, without any fuss. Afterall, he just could not leave them on the steps of the building like some abandoned baby in front of a hospital and he refused to get caught smuggling books back into the library!

Over the two-year period, he had come to be very friendly with the head librarian who had helped him obtain books on inter-library loan. They talked frequently about football, the Troubles, and books. Perhaps he could tell this Mr Sloan the simple truth—that he was returning what he had 'borrowed'.

But he had frequented Mr Sloan sufficiently to know that the man was decent, ethically sound. He was not sure about his solution as he knew the minimum reproach would be that he had been selfish and prevented other pupils from having the same advantage as himself. He did not think the library would fine him or even make a big fuss—after all, there were bombings going on and people being shot at regularly in the street. The books were no big deal.

Paul filled a rucksack with the thirty-eight volumes and, one Saturday morning in July, he slipped out of the house and made his way up the Donegall Road. He went through the heavy wooden doors, past the front desk, to Mr Sloan's small office where the chief librarian was sat at his large, solid mahogany desk. He saw Paul through the glass part of the door and waved him to come in. The man looked immediately at the bulging and heavy-looking rucksack: "An' what have ya got there, Son?"

Paul hesitated too long.

"Mr Sloan… Mr Sloan… I found a pile o' books in the entry where we keep the bonfire wood. I think they were goin' to burn them on the twelfth but they all have the library stamp so I thought I'd bring them to you."

"Well, let's have a look at them."

Paul put his rucksack on the floor and then made five uneven piles of books on the librarian's desk. The latter began looking through each one without saying a word. Paul was starting to doubt himself and wished he had just told the simple truth. He wanted to flee. The man finished his examination of the books and returned to his seat opposite the standing boy.

"You didn't take these books yerself then, did you? I mean, you didn't steal them?"

"Sir, I… I…"

The man wanted the boy to tell the truth.

"Come on Son, spit it out!"

"Yes, I did! I know… I mean, I knew I would bring them back, sir."

"But effectively, you stole them."

"Effectively… I did. I'm sorry."

"Did ya pass yar A-levels?"

"I did."

"So ya'll be off to Blighty, then?"

Paul had never heard the term 'Blighty' before but he understood it meant leaving this island. He nodded.

"I'll tell ya what, Son. Because you brought the books back; because you admitted you took them; an' because you said you were sorry… I am letting you off."

Paul closed his eyes and sighed deeply.

"Thank you, sir… Mr Sloan, thank you!"

"But you have to promise me something: you see, you could have a great future… but you must promise me, you will never do something like this again."

"I promise. It will never happen again."

"Off you go, then."

Paul was about to leave the office when Mr Sloan called him back. He was holding a copy of a book of criticism on *Sons and Lovers* that was on the top of one of the piles of books.

"Just on the off-chance, Son: you didn't by any chance take a copy of D.H. Lawrence's *Sons and Lovers*? It was a first edition and signed by D.H. Lawrence himself on the inner cover. Now, worth a fair bit of money. It has disappeared from the library."

"No sir, I didn't. I never needed any of the actual texts so I wouldn't have been interested."

Paul thought for a moment before adding:

"An' besides that, ya couldn't sell it if it belonged to the library because it would have the library stamp on several different pages."

"You're a smart lad! An' I don't believe ya took it, I have other suspicions."

Mr Sloan looked beyond Paul to the lady on the front desk. He screwed up his eyes.

"Okay, Son, off ya go now. And good luck!"

Paul was happy to be outside the building and on his way down the Donegall Road. He said to himself that the *Sons and Lovers* thief was probably a librarian who knew the value of a Lawrence signed first edition. In that case, he was convinced that the library would never see the book again. He became conscious of the rucksack slipping from his shoulder and which now felt as light as his soul as he began cantering down the Donegall Road on a bright new July morning.

The Departure

Robert Craig sat in his mother's armchair looking into the cold, swept-clean hearth. His mother had left to go to her sister's house in England a month previously. Her nerves were bad because of the 'Troubles,' and the endless bombings and shootings which punctuated their daily lives. They were living in 1972—the bloodiest year of the conflict, a conflict that forced her husband to take the difficult decision to leave Belfast. He sent his wife on first, as he stayed with his son who was completing his A-levels.

It was the second week in July and Robert had just received his positive exam results and with them came a place in an English university. He was relieved and happy. Northern Ireland was finished for their family and he was resolved to put at least ten years between this moment and the moment he would come back to visit Ulster—if ever he was to come back to visit 'the oven you were baked in,' as local people put it. Many others had gone before. Robert's family, as well as the community, had been shattered, irreparably. He sat back in the armchair to savour this moment of departure, of escape. It felt as if he had earned it and there would be no regrets in leaving the boys he had grown up with who were now entangled in the web of violence he would have the luxury of contemplating from a distance. This was a new and welcome experience.

As he sat in silence, Robert heard a mouse scraping against the thick, superimposed layers of embossed wallpaper as it scrambled up the crumbling wall. He heard it stop at some obstacle blocking its ascension. It was momentarily trapped. He reached out and banged on the wall at the point where he believed the mouse to be searching for an exit. Bingo! He heard the creature lose its grip and fall to the bottom of the vertical space it was attempting to explore. It would remain in the disintegrating house long after his departure. There would be no other human occupant—except perhaps for phantom squatters—as the place, like all the houses in the area, was due for demolition.

Robert looked at his watch: his father would be home soon from his tour of vigilante duty. This involved patrolling the neighbourhood with a large wooden stick for protection. All those of eighteen and above were involved in this neighbourhood watch although Robert had so far been left out because of his A-levels. There was still a lot of respect amongst the locals for 'education,' although it was more recognised today as a way out than a way up. His father's duty lasted for three hours twice a week, just after dark. Younger men had a later shift. When they toppled a bus to erect a barricade at the junction with Shaftesbury Square, his father still remained on patrol. It was the young men who perched on the side of the bus, looking defiantly down the Donegall Pass towards the RUC post.

Robert rose and went into the scullery where the sink was piled high with dirty dishes. This was his chore and he had to get it out of the way before his father came home. The latter did all of the cooking. This was the case even when his mother was at home. It had become the norm after the wife fell through the glass roof covering the scullery as she attempted to whitewash the back wall. Her recuperation period lasted for years and so Robert became used to his father's fry-ups and Sunday dinners which were always too greasy and floating in gravy. Dishes were never a pleasure to do so he inevitably waited until well after dinner to wash the day's quota. He had to boil up lots of hot water first.

As he was organising the plates and waiting for the kettle to boil, Robert became aware of unusually loud noises coming from outside. He looked up through the skylight to see lines criss-crossing the stars. In different circumstances these might be taken for the trails of shooting stars but Robert recognised them as the tails of tracer bullets. He stood and watched as the piercing sounds became more and more distinct. Suddenly, he heard the hall door being thrust open and he turned round quickly to look through the window behind him where he saw the dishevelled figure of his father rush into the centre of the room and call his name. Robert left the dishes and went back into the sitting-room.

"What's wrong?" he asked worriedly. Unlike his friends in the street, Robert never called his father 'da' as he knew it would be taken as a lack of respect. In fact, he avoided using any epithet to describe the kindred bond between them. He had not yet worked out why this was the case.

Looking at his son anxiously, the father pushed his mass of thick, black hair backwards with both hands. He then picked up the stick, which he had placed momentarily against his thigh, and stood it against the wall behind the settee.

"That won't be much good to us tonight!"

"Why, what's happenin'?"

"There's a lot o' talk about Taigs comin' up the Pass from the Markets—an' they'll not be comin' wi' sticks!" He looked at his son fixedly and realised immediately that he had said the wrong thing. He could see the fear in his son's eyes and regretted his words.

"It's alright, Son… they'll not get up to here." And in a gentler, almost caressing tone, he reassured his son further, "We'll be alright. There's no risk… more talk than anything else—sure ya know what people are like."

"I'll just finish the dishes an' then make a cup o' tea."

"Aye thanks, Son, I could do wi' a cup o' tea!"

Mr Craig had just begun tidying up in the sitting-room, hanging up his coat, arranging cushions and chairs, when a huge explosion was heard not far off. He went quickly to the front door and secured the bolt. He did the same to the snib on the glass-panelled door which gave on to the sitting-room. Robert heard his movements and understood what was going on but he continued with the dishes regardless. He still heard the bullets screaming overhead but felt relatively safe. No one would come to kill them. The Craigs had never done anyone any harm.

Then he thought about the time his friend Geordie McManus had taken him to a dance in the Markets area. He had not wanted to go as he knew the reputation of the area but Geordie had said there was nothing to worry about as he knew everybody in the club, and so he went along. He was standing at the counter when three boys he could see in the mirror behind the bar, approached and stood directly behind him. When he turned to say 'hello', they started punching and kicking him until Geordie rescued him by pushing him out of the hall to the staircase. He had had no time to be afraid and he hardly felt the blows hitting him. But he had done nothing to antagonise them—at least nothing he was aware of. Now, his new suit was covered in his own blood. They knew he was a Protestant, just as most people in working-class Northern Ireland believe they can tell the next man's religion just by looking at him. He did not want to be a victim a second time.

When the dishes were finished, Robert made the tea and carried it in to his father. They both drank silently, staring into the grate. The noise outside would come and go but it definitely seemed to be getting louder each time. There came another bomb blast from even closer than before and the screeching sounds of tyres as cars sped up the Donegall Road. People were shouting commands to each other. His father turned the lights out.

"I think, Son, we might be better in the toilet."

Robert knew his father was not a coward—he had even been a boxer for several years. He was just a sensible man being protective. It was obvious that if the Fenians managed to fight their way up the Pass to Shaftesbury Square, then their street was next in line. But he could not see them getting past the RUC barracks which had been well fortified after three years of being targeted by the Paras. Still, they would do better to move to the outside toilet which stood back-to-back with the next street and was therefore sheltered even if the front of the house was torched. Robert knew what torched houses looked like—his own side had started it and now it was quite a common technique to remove the 'unwanted'.

Father and son moved through the scullery which the former had rebuilt after his wife's accident. It was now a sturdy brick edifice with a skylight and a gap which separated it from the toilet and coalhole. Mr Craig had left this gap in order to have access to the roof which sometimes needed maintenance. They stood together here, looking up at the stars and the screaming tracers. Robert propped his back against the wall and although he was already taller than his father, he had the impression that the latter was leaning over him, perhaps in an effort to offer him more protection. Robert looked admiringly at his broad shoulders which enveloped his son like a shield. When the noise of bullets suddenly increased, the boy lowered his head so that the sky was completely blocked out by the bulk of his father's dominant body.

"Why don't ya sit on the toilet son, if yar tired?" the man said gently.

"I'm okay, thanks."

The father attempted to distract his son by indulging in small talk—football, which he did not know much about and then boxing, which he knew a lot about. Cassius Clay was his current favourite although he still had not got round to calling him Mohamed Ali. The father himself had reached a certain degree of notoriety in that field and was still respected because of it in the neighbourhood. He had been very fast, with a dense muscular mass and very broad shoulders.

He repeated again to his son: "Remember, if ya ever get into a fight, hit first and ask questions later. Even if it turns out you are in the wrong. Better to regret that you hit someone than to regret that you didn't!"

This seemed to be a strange philosophy to his son whose natural inclination was exactly the opposite. He looked at his father's face in wonder. The only evidence of his boxing past were the thickened and deformed earlobes—cauliflower ears, as he called them. The man would remain a mystery, a strange creature living on the other side of a widening gulf which would probably never be breached.

The firing outside intensified for a moment and Robert looked again at his father's manly physique and thick, jet-black hair. His youthfulness made his son suddenly resentful, "You know, all that time you spent working in England—why did you not take us with you? I would rather have grown up in England."

The words rang out like so many shots and the man stood stunned at this reproach.

"Aye, I could've brought yous all over but yar ma was against it Son. Ya know what she's like—her an' her cronies. This is the first time she ever wanted to leave Belfast. It took the 'Troubles' to shift 'er."

"I hardly knew you when I was growin' up." The boy was still vexed.

"I did try Son, an' she was thinkin' about it seriously at one point but then she fell through that friggin' roof! It just wasn't meant to be."

Robert surveyed the concrete roof over the scullery which his father had constructed. He was good with his hands. There was certainly truth in what he was saying but the boy felt that it was not the only truth. He suspected his father wanted to be on his own, to live a life outside his marriage and family.

Mr Craig sensed his son's now quiet animosity but he was a very pragmatic person: no use crying over spilled milk was his current philosophy. His son would have to get over it and move on with his own life. He would find out for himself. Besides, a man does not have to justify his life to his children.

It was the father's turn to look up at the stars. He had no regrets. He had divided his life into two compartments: there was the family man who ruled his home responsibly and with harsh discipline; and there was the private man who had followed his work wherever it took him. This man was single in his ways which he pursued with avid pleasure. He was a man whose company women enjoyed and which they would eagerly seek. His son should not resent him for this. He should think about his own choices to come.

"Yar a worrier, Son!" was his conclusion.

Robert looked into the man's small, intensely brown eyes which seemed to contract and harden. He waited for his father to continue.

"Son, I'll tell ya something, an' you mark my words: Ya see ma hair? I've still got all ma hair an' its jet black. Ya know why that is? Well, I'll tell ya why: I never worried about a single thing in my life. That's the God's truth, not a thing, an' I advise you to do the same."

"We're not the same."

"Aye, I know that, Son! Yar like my brother Sid. Nigh he was a worrier! Smart fella too. He died thin as a rake an' bald as a coot. A bundle o' nerves, he was, an' it took him to an early grave. I'm tellin' ya, Son, it's not worth it. You've only got one life—make the most of it!"

The night outside was becoming noisier again. His father stopped speaking and they both listened to the sound of machine-guns. He thought of the irony of the situation: men in the streets trying to murder one another whilst his father was coaxing him not to worry about anything! He could not help but smile. His father read the smile as approval to go on speaking. The irony was lost on him.

"That's right Son, better to laugh about things! Don't let them get to you. Ya know, your problem is that yar too smart for yar own good! To tell the truth, I don't know where you got yar brains from—not from yar ma, that's for sure! There was Sid, as I said… hell of a smart fella—always readin' books an' wouldn't talk to ya, wouldn't talk to anybody. He kept himself to himself—wasn't interested in other people's business or at least 'e didn't show any interest. Wouldn't spend Christmas either! Tight as a duck's arse—wouldn't even buy ya a pint!"

Mr Craig suddenly became lost in childhood memories and drifted off into the world of his lost brothers and sisters. They were all either dead or had become estranged. He wondered if he should have kept contact with them, especially Horace in Australia. No, we all have to walk our own path and there was no sympathy to be wasted on himself, standing now in a Belfast toilet with his almost grown-up son. Besides, they would be moving on soon, leaving the killing fields behind them.

When he looked at his son again, he saw that the latter was staring fixedly at the black coal which had spilled from the coal-hole. He would have to stop this brooding!

"Stop taking things so seriously, Son! In another few days we'll be away from here and ya'll be at university. Ya'll have a great time!"

Robert looked at him expectantly. He was sure this last subject would lead his father into more unwanted advice. He was not wrong.

"Remember Son, it's the same wi' women. Don't let yarself get bogged down—you have time enough for that. Enjoy life! Love 'em and leave 'em Son: that's the best bit of advice I can give ya. Aye, love 'em and leave 'em."

Robert reflected upon this 'manly' advice as he stared at the figure who had given him life. Just how far had he followed his own advice? He had married young and had four children, all in the run of things. And then? How many women had this man loved and left? Probably a good few. And it did not cost him a worry. Robert felt sorry for these women he did not know. He half-smiled this time: after all, it was really none of his business.

It took the father a few minutes to realise that he had perhaps said too much and that his son might be putting two and two together and coming up with both four and five. Safer to put an end to the conversation.

"I just mean, Son, that you'll have yar own life to live an' all I can say is that ya should make the most of it while ya can. As they say, yar a long time dead."

For a moment, Robert was conscious that a silence stood between them—perhaps a silence that—even if he could find them—the right words would never fill. They both felt ill at ease and began to look upwards at the bullets still tracing their stoical route, criss-crossing the sky in fine streaks pulled across the dancing play of light and dark.

Robert did not want to resent his father. In many ways, he admired him: this pugnacious, good-looking, intelligent, working-class man who had pushed his way through life, rolling with the punches and handing out quite a few. In his own way, he was a loner, self-contained, an outsider different from the other men but conforming to an inherited notion of masculinity which he regretted not being able to pass on. He was fortunate to live in a world beyond compromise and doubt, forever his own man. And yet, as Robert looked at him, he realised that this man would not hesitate to give his life for his son. For this he could be eternally thankful.

This odd, blood-bound couple stood for a long time together in the cooling air of the July night, sporadically exchanging banalities, snippets of life. Despite their obvious differences, Robert felt suddenly very close to this man who would willingly step between him and the world, bend over him protectively, despite his professed survival strategy.

The hours passed. They remained in the protection of the toilet until the noise abated and partially collapsed into the normal stuttering of sporadic individual gunfire which became more and more distant. Time for bed. The father ushered his son back into the house and towards the stairs. He checked the doors and windows while his son went up to his bedroom.

Robert kept the light off as he undressed. He stood for a brief moment looking out the back window before climbing into bed. He listened to his father's heavy, laboured footsteps coming up the stairs. There was a hesitant pause at his bedroom door.

"Goodnight, Son," came the soft words.

"Goodnight… Goodnight, Da… Dad." He thought he could hear his father smile. There was another moment's hesitation and then the latter went into his own bedroom and Robert listened as he climbed heavily into his creaking bed.

Robert lay thinking about England and his future university life. He was happy to get away from Belfast. He was happy also to have just spent several hours with his father standing in the shelter of the toilet open to the sky. Happy finally, to have made the acquaintance of someone who had, up to this evening, essentially been a well-intentioned enigma—a benevolent stranger to him.

The Girl from Stranmillis

Herbie's family had moved into the street from the bottom of the Donegall Pass because they felt that they were too exposed to marauding gangs from the Markets area putting pressure on locals to leave 'in the interests of both communities.' A lot of his friends' families had already fled the area to go to new housing estates far from the city centre, but his mother had refused that option.

When they moved to the Row, Herbie was sixteen and about to leave school in June without any prospect of employment. He was in charge of two younger sisters he had to look out for. The world had become a dangerous place, especially for young girls in their early teens. The family moved next door to the Bells who had only one son—a seventeen-year old known by everyone as 'Dinger'. The latter had left school the year before and had been unemployed since, but managed to survive doing the odd job, scavenging, pilfering and, more recently, robbing houses in the well-off Malone Road area. Due to proximity, Dinger and Herbie inevitably became friends, although the latter still had to prove himself.

After a quick lunch which his mother had prepared for him, Herbie was enticed into the street by the sound of

Dinger's voice. The latter was talking to Cal, another out of work seventeen-year old who had grown up with Dinger and looked to him to make all the decisions in his life. On seeing him, they stopped speaking for a moment until Dinger vouched that Herbie was now one of them. Cal went on:

"She's always in the rose garden after school… about four o'clock. We still have time to get up there this afternoon, if ya want to. Just the two of us—or even three." Cal looked at Herbie who in turn looked at Dinger.

"What's happenin'?"

"We were up the Gardies last week an' met this girl. She's a bit fat but she has big tits. She took us into the Puzzies—there were four of us an' we all rode 'er."

Dinger was keen on the venture and looked at Herbie for an enthusiastic response.

"I don't know. I'm supposed to be choppin' sticks for my ma this afternoon." The other boys looked at one another. This was not a good start for Herbie.

"Aye, alright, I can do the sticks in the mornin'."

The boys set out briskly towards Botanic Gardens. Herbie and Cal talked most of the time but Dinger was lost in thought: he had to come up with a Plan B just in case the girl was not there. He would be on the lookout for delivery lorries—laundry and furniture vans were always a good bet, but they would have to be off the main road as it was too risky otherwise.

They crossed the central stretch of grass field from the side entrance and went straight to the rose garden where they saw a girl in school uniform bending over some roses to take in the perfume.

"That's her. Bet ya she's not wearin' any knickers," said Cal, "she wasn't last week."

"What's 'er name?" asked Herbie.

"I don't know! Nobody ast her name an' she never told us."

The boys approached the girl from behind but she was not at all surprised to see them when they appeared and said 'Hello'. She turned and smiled, and then returned the greeting as if she was happy they had come. Herbie did not think she was very attractive. She urged the boys to smell the roses and they bent over obediently.

"That's not a smell they can bottle, no matter how hard they try," she said, looking at the new boy, Herbie.

"Yar right there! By the way, I forgot to ask ya yar name last week—what are ya called?" Cal decided that it would be polite to show some interest in the girl. She thought for a moment before replying: "Nathalie. And you?"

"I'm Sammy, an' this is Robbie an' Davey," said the boy, introducing his two friends.

"D'ya fancy a wee walk through the Puzzies?"

"I would get scratched and get my uniform dirty." The boys looked at each other but she had no intention of disappointing them for long.

"But you can come to my house as my parents have gone to Portstewart and won't be back until after tea. I live just over there," she said, pointing to the high hedge which enclosed the back of the first house which ran parallel to the park and led up to the large gates of the Stranmillis entrance.

"I can change out of these school clothes," the girl smiled again at them before moving towards the small side exit which ran from the rose garden. The boys followed, remaining about a yard behind.

"I'm first jockey," said Dinger, under his breath.

"Second!" said Cal. Herbie just looked at the girl's plumpish silhouette. Apart from not finding her attractive—as well as being overweight, she had freckles and disturbingly thick lips—Herbie was starting to have serious reservations about what he was getting into.

Dinger seemed to be aware of this, and so put his arm around the younger boy's neck and whispered into his ear: "It's alright, ya don't look at the fireplace when yer pokin' the fire, do ya?" They laughed quietly in growing complicity.

They entered the house via the back door, hidden by the high hedge. Nathalie said she was going upstairs to get changed but when she was in her bedroom, she soon called for one of the boys to come up. Dinger looked at the other two: "That's me lads… duty calls!" He glanced at Cal: "Go through the cupboards, drawers an' so on—see if there is anything worth pinchin'." Turning to the other boy he said, "An' you watch the front door—we don't want her ma an' da comin' home unexpectedly. Okay, Herbie? I mean 'Davey'!"

Herbie nodded and watched Dinger lightly climb the stairs before turning his attention to the front door.

Cal set about overturning objects, displacing cushions and seats, opening and closing drawers and rummaging through boxes or whatever diverse containers he could lay his hands on.

"Not much aroun' here," he said as he looked at Herbie disappointedly.

"I'll try the kitchen… anyway, I'm fuckin' starvin'!"

Herbie stood behind the curtain, looking up the street through the large bay window. He was afraid someone would come home—especially if he was up the stairs at the time. He knew the others would get out quickly and leave him to face the music. He had to be ready to climb out the back window. But his thoughts were interrupted by Cal returning to the sitting-room with a half-eaten leg of chicken in one hand and a saltcellar in the other.

"Ya want some? There's plenty in the fridge," indicating the direction by a backward flick of the head. Herbie shook his head. He certainly had no appetite for food. In fact, he was starting to feel a bit out of sorts.

"Didn't find any dough in there."

They both fell silent as they listened to the slow, heavy steps descending the stairs. When he reached the doorway, Dinger was fastening his belt and pulling up his flies in a gesture of triumph. Cal let him enjoy the moment before thrusting the chicken and salt into his hands:

"My turn!"

Dinger eagerly tore off a piece of chicken with his teeth while scanning the room for signs that it had been given a good going over.

"Did 'e find any plunder?" Dinger ate with his mouth open so that Herbie noticed his sharp incisors for the first time.

"Not as far as I know." Dinger went into the kitchen and began rummaging around for himself. He found a jar containing coins which he quietly slipped into his pocket before returning to the sitting-room. Cal was already coming down the stairs.

"That was fast!" said Dinger.

"She was lyin' waitin' on the bed... it doesn't take me long. Fuckin' big tits on 'er!" He winked at Herbie who was now becoming very agitated as his turn had arrived. Cal looked at his trousers before tucking his shirt neatly into them.

"What's that in yer back pocket?" Dinger never missed a trick.

"It's a cigarette case I foun' in a drawer in the kitchen." He handed it over to the elder boy who scrutinised it and tapped it with his index finger.

"I think it's silver. We'll take it to the pawn shop. There must be a few other wee silver things in the kitchen—check again. An' then check that other downstairs room—and the glass place." He looked over at Herbie as he lifted his head in a quick, upward movement: "Away ya go, Son!" Herbie did not move.

"What's wrong with ya? Are you scared?"

"I'm not scared... just don't fancy her."

"Listen, ya don't look a gift horse in the mouth!" Dinger was full of these ready-made formulas.

"Aye, but..."

"Have ya done it before?" Herbie again hesitated.

"Ya haven't, have ya? It's alright—she'll lead ya through. She knows what she wants. Ya won't get another chance like this one, Son."

They could hear Cal turning things over in the next room. The girl called from upstairs: "Come on up Davey!"

"See, she wants ya up there—Davey! There'll be no comeback. Away ya go!" and Dinger pushed him gently toward the stairs.

Herbie climbed the latter slowly. Perhaps he could just touch her, maybe squeeze her, explore areas he had never explored before. She was softly singing in her bed and her voice beckoned him, leading him to her bedroom. When he reached the door, he could see her lying on her single divan, naked from the waist down with her bra pulled above her breasts. He focussed on her black-wavy hair which spilled across the white pillow.

"Come over and sit on the bed." Nathalie made a friendly gesture to him. She knew that he was the type who needed coaxing. He sat down beside her, still looking at her hair.

"Give me your hand!" Herbie obeyed. She took his hand and rubbed it over her nipples, uttering little snatches of pleasure before pulling it down to her pubic hair. She began rubbing herself softly at first and then frantically, expertly using his hand until it was almost numb and she cried out ecstatically.

Herbie looked at her closed eyes, shifting under the lids. He had gone far enough. She opened them and looked directly into his eyes: "I want you to come inside!" He was mesmerised by her gaze but saw something frightening in those dark-brown, almost black eyes. They appealed to him in a bitterly mocking way. She held his hand to her sex again whilst slipping her other hand on to his zipper. He moved away but left his hand in hers and moved it voluntarily this time to give her pleasure. The girl's body writhed and shook until she released another savage cry of sharp gratification. This time he pulled his hand away from her—it gave off an unpleasant odour which he did not recognise.

"I don't want to come inside you. Maybe next time."

"You can come alone, if you like. I can meet you at the weekend in the rose garden, okay?"

"That sounds like a good idea." Herbie knew he would never see the girl again. He went downstairs and was greeted triumphantly on arrival by the others. He had quickly pulled his shirt out of his jeans and partially undone his zipper to fool the others and now began rearranging his clothes.

"Don't forget yer flies!" said Cal. Both boys looked at him admiringly.

"She seems to have enjoyed it!" said Dinger, with a wink.

"Did yous find anything else down here?"

"We foun' a fiver an' a silver cigarette-case an' a silver lighter! Not bad, eh?"

Before he could answer, Dinger said they should leave through the backdoor before anyone came home to find them there. They shouted 'Goodbye' to Nathalie and left the house. Once outside, the boys quickly retraced their steps to the rose garden and then continued along the path to the central green where they sat down for a moment in the late sunshine. Dinger took out the silver items and all the money. He divided the coins into three with a promise to split the note later. Cal was to take the silver items to the local pawn shop. Dinger laughed as he looked at Cal, saying: "Ya know, it was his first time! She was certainly screamin' for more!"

Herbie enjoyed his newly found credibility but was quick to change the subject as he did not want to go into any detail concerning what actually went on in the bedroom.

"D'ya think it was a good idea to take those things—if she squeals, we'll be in trouble."

"D'ya think she's gonna tell her da' that she had three boys in his house? He knows the score. Don't be daft! She'd have to admit she bucked the three of us—what d'ya think her da would say to her? No way! No comeback!"

Herbie still looked sceptical.

"Luck, they're rich—ya saw the house, didn't ya? The loose coins are just for messages an' the fiver she can say she bought something with. They probably won't even notice the lighter and case—bet the Da doesn't smoke anymore – probably good livin'. Anyway, she'll get out of it if she has to. She's not stupid. She's just… what's that word?" Dinger looked at Cal.

"A nymphomaniac," Cal took his time pronouncing it.

"What's that?"

"Somebody who likes getting rid all the time," said Dinger.

"Like us!" said Cal.

"Aye, except ya have to be a girl to be a nymphomaniac." Dinger seemed to be an expert on the subject.

Herbie was intrigued by the word and the fact that boys could not be nymphomaniacs. He decided that Dinger knew what he was talking about and that Nathalie would probably not say anything. She could even spin her parents a yarn about leaving the door open when she went to the park and somebody must have been watching her and so entered the house. There were endless possibilities. This was probably not the first time she had been in this situation.

He lay back and closed his eyes to feel the warmth of the sun on his face. His fingers still gave off that unpleasant smell which the others, thankfully, did not notice. He cusped one hand around the other to contain the smell, just in case.

Dinger was certainly right—there would be no comeback. That was the important thing. If nobody finds out then, in a way, it did not really happen. Nevertheless, he resolved not to return to the rose garden within the near future, the others could do what they want. He looked over to the water fountain—he would have to get rid of that pungent odour on his hands.

The Hard Man

Sammy Gourlay was born right at the end of the nineteenth-century, which meant that he was too young to join up at the start of the First World War but managed to lie about his age in order to get into uniform before the real battle of the Somme got underway. Before going to the Somme, Sammy began serving his time as an apprentice metal-worker in the Belfast shipyard where his stocky build soon thickened into a powerful physique that put off boys of his age from challenging him to a fight. But he was no giant—only five foot eight—and his lack of height contributed greatly to his survival in the trenches where the tallest men were the first to be 'popped off' by the enemy.

When the men around him, whom he had known only a matter of days, began to fall in the thick of battle, Sammy quickly felt a burning hatred for the Germans. He had always hated Catholics before he joined up, and added the arrogant English to his list because of the squaddies he came into contact with when off-duty. He got into fist fights with many of them and usually came out victorious. But Sammy soon began to hate even the soldiers with him in the trenches—no sooner did he get to know them than they would be sprawled over the barbed wire of No Man's Land. He especially hated the officers who sent the men over the top. In fact, Sammy's universe became peopled solely by human beings he did not like and it was with lust that he ravaged the body of anyone who dared stand bayonet to bayonet with him. He lost the notion of 'friend and foe'—there was just the enemy beside him and the enemy opposite, and he knew which one had to go first.

Towards the end of the Somme battle, and after months of ferocious fighting, Sammy was hit in the face by shrapnel and consequently lost a chunk of cheek and his left eye. It happened as he juked for cover moving forward into a maelstrom of bullets, shells and scraps of burning metal. He fell behind what looked like the hind quarters of a horse and continued firing with his good eye while the right side of his face streamed blood and fell away from him. He turned back only when the whistle blew to recall the men to the trenches. An officer pulled him over and into the mud which is when he was baptised with his new name—Cyclopes.

The doctor treating him told him that Cyclopes was a fierce one-eyed giant who defeated all of his enemies. Sam thought this implied that he would soon be sent back to the frontline. He knew he only needed one good eye to shoot Germans. But he was wrong, and after several weeks, he was sent first of all to a hospital in the south of England and then shipped back to Belfast. For months he wore a patch over his left eye which made him look even more savage so that people would get out of his path as he walked down the street. When the war was over, he was given a glass eye which toned down his ferociousness but increased the demented instability of his gaze.

Sammy went back to better paid work in Harland and Wolff's where he was now employed as a hod carrier. The job suited and reinforced his physique where a low centre of gravity, powerful arms and shoulders, ensured that he could walk up and down planks all day, carrying massive weights to welders and mechanics. The skin on his hands became so thick that he could feel nothing. He never stopped to talk to fellow workers and rarely stopped to drink water and his aloofness maintained his unwelcoming disposition. It was a serious risk to try to befriend him. He was to everyone a muted character who shunned civilities.

For many years he lived alone until one day he asked his neighbour to marry him. Janet also lived on her own as her husband never returned from the Somme. She tried to raise two young boys without a fater but it was becoming increasingly more difficult. Sammy took the three of them in and raised the boys as his own, which meant that they never uttered a word out of place. Through time they grew more and more like their benefactor, nurturing a feeling of bitter animosity which smouldered beneath a seemingly indifferent exterior.

When World War II came around, the boys joined up with Sammy's grudging benediction. He was jealous of them because he knew that the army would reject him despite the fact that, in his mid-forties, his body was in prime condition. The Cyclopes was convinced that he could still handle any living man.

Whilst the presence of the boys had irritated him intensely, their absence now drove him to distraction. His wife deeply regretted the departure of her sons as well as the muted enmity of her husband. She would have preferred to live alone, as solitude in the presence of another is made acutely more painful. She hated her husband now and cursed the army for not taking him instead of her boys. Her boys did not return home after the war.

Months passed, then years. Sammy spent every evening in the pub, drinking alone but listening to men around him. If he did not like what he overheard, he would give the person the chance to withdraw his remark; if they did not do so, he would pommel them to the ground. Men learned to keep their voices down when Sammy was within earshot.

Young men home on leave from the war unwittingly became his worst enemy. He expected them never to talk about what they saw or did at the front, and certainly never to make the slightest boast about their encounters with Germans. But often, these young men proved to be different from their World War I counterparts. They were more loud-mouthed and boisterous. Sensing Sammy's growing irritation, the barman would often intervene to tell them to keep their voices down but on one occasion Sammy jumped up and grabbed one man by the throat whilst two others tried to tear him away. They jumped on Sammy who, being too close, could not get a punch in and instead bit one of the men in the arm. He tried to take a lump out of a second man but the three were quickly out of the door screaming the word 'animal' as they left. Sammy was then barred from the Albion Bar.

He consequently changed public house and routine. He stopped going to the pub during the week and reserved the weekend for his drinking. Sammy had become well-known in the Row and when he was seen in a pub there was always a respectable space invisibly marked out around him. He was both feared and unwanted.

His reputation continued well into the fifties, with other men avoiding his company, both at work and outside. He enjoyed this form of recognition, it made him want to stand up and roar, to issue a fearsome, one-eyed challenge to the world.

Friday night would always see Sammy stagger home from the pub around midnight. He, who had always kept his words to himself, took to cursing loudly as he stumbled past the quiet houses in the street. If he saw a light in a bedroom window, he would stop and yell up at the man in the house: "If yer a man, ya'll come down an' fight!"

It was rare for anyone to react but often a woman would pull the sash window upwards and tell Sammy that he ought to be ashamed of himself keeping people out of their beds at this time of night, and to take himself off home. This was usually sufficient to quieten the lust for bare-knuckle fighting that Sammy's lightning hammer blows had made him so famous for.

It happened that, one Friday evening, Sammy stopped as usual under bedroom windows to harangue his neighbours: "If yar a man ya'll come down here an' fight!" But he got no response. He wavered and wobbled his way down the street until he was almost home, spluttering out:

"Ya bunch o' cowardly bastards!" Then he stood for a shaky moment outside Davey Scott's house and looked up at the bedroom window where the light was still on. Davey was a strong, well-built man in his thirties who also worked in the shipyard. He neither liked nor respected Sammy, but knew of his reputation and that he had come through the war.

When Sammy shouted up for the younger man to come down and fight, Davey said to his wife as he went over to the window to pull the blind slightly aside: "There's that stupid bastard again. Every Friday night it's the same thing. They should put 'im to sleep!"

Sammy stood watching the window. He could see the other man's shape thrown up against the blind by the bedside lamp. It seemed huge against the light.

"Scott, ya wee bastard! Come out here an' show 's yar a man!"

Davey stood undecided. He let the blind fly up and opened the window.

"Fuck off Sammy! Away home to yar bed, ya stupid oul gat!"

"Come down here an' say that! If ya don't come down, I'll smash yar fuckin' window!"

This was enough for Davey. He put his vest and trousers back on, fastened his belt buckle, and headed downstairs where he quickly laced up his boots. When he opened the front door and stepped over the threshold, Sammy threw a punch at him which Davey had been expecting. He pulled his body quickly backwards and Sammy's fist hit the brick wall. The power behind the swing carried him off his feet and he found himself looking up at this giant, outlined against the brightness of the stars. He tried to scramble on to his feet but before he could get beyond his knees, Davey hit him several times in the face with his broad, bony fists. The fight did not last very long and Sammy's prostrate body was soon sprawled across the pavement. He did not make more than a slight moaning sound; the features of his face already barely distinguishable as he stared fixedly at the heavens with his one partially closed eye.

"I'll get ya home, ya stupid oul bastard, yar too oul for this sort o' thing." Davey raised the heap of bloodied flesh that had been his adversary and carried him to his house where he helped Sammy's wife put the older man to bed. He felt no hatred of the man who had disturbed the lives of neighbours every Friday night. Sammy lay on the bed a pathetic figure, but not even a groan came from him now. This forced a certain respect from the younger man.

Sammy remained in bed for several days and did not return to work—it was almost time to retire anyway and he did not have a problem in bringing it forward a couple of months. He slept for long periods every day. One afternoon, he woke up to see his glass eye sitting on the bedside table—it had been knocked out of its socket during the fight and Davey had found it in the street on the Saturday morning. It took him a few days to return it to its rightful owner. The glass eye was badly scored but sat staring fixedly at Sammy, communicating what seemed to be a final, undeniable truth: Sammy had fought his last battle. He had been a good soldier but the noise of the battlefield had now been silenced forever. He was relieved that he would never again need to face the enemy but the overpowering shame of his final defeat kept him nailed to his bed for much longer than was necessary to heal physically. He listened to the heavy silence of the bedroom which informed him that he was now lost to the company of men.

The Will

"Hi ya, Joe! Ya weren't in today?"

"No, had to do a run out to Strabane. Why are ya askin'?"

"There was a man roun' luckin' for ya."

"What did he want?"

"Well, he didn't want to say much—just said he was luckin' for Joseph McKinley. I said ya wud be away on the lorry an' he said he wud come back again."

"An' he didn't say what he wanted?"

"He said he was from a solicitor's outfit in town. I asked him if it was bad news an' he said no, on the contrary… that ya might have come into a bit o' money. Sounds to me like a will or something—ya'll be buyin' the drinks soon!" Joe was gracious enough not to point out that he usually bought the drinks anyway.

"Do us a favour Billy, keep this ta yarself, will ya? At least until I know what it's about, okay?"

"Aye, no problem Joe."

Billy and Joe were next door neighbours as well as being close friends. Billy was unemployed so Joe would take him out in the lorry with him, just for a bit of company and to give Billy something to do from time to time. He was relieved that his wife had not been at home today to receive his visitor. It could turn out to be nothing at all but his friend had done the right thing in coming down to the pub to tell him what had happened. For this discretion, Billy had earned himself a good pint of Guinness.

The next day was Saturday, so no one would be arriving at his door and Joe would have the weekend to mull over this story about coming into a bit of money. He had a good idea what the source of the money might be but he hoped that he was wrong for it could mean a lot of trouble at home and there was nothing in this world that Joe loved more and wanted to protect, than his wife and three children.

Joe was a very good-looking man of forty who worked for a transport firm. He had to make frequent trips to England, usually around the Coventry area, to drop off his loads and pick up others to bring to Northern Ireland. He inevitably spent his evenings in pubs where, being a very sociable person, he mixed and chatted with many of the locals. It happened on several occasions that he spent the night in a lady's house rather than in his usual digs. He always rang home from a telephone box—this was in the eighties when mobile phones were thankfully not common possessions.

It happened that one night, Joe went home with a very attractive and intelligent woman who was six or seven years older than himself. They got on particularly well together and Joe began spending all his midweek stopovers with June, as the lady was called, thus banking his weekly travel allowance and eventually providing more for his loved ones. The relationship rapidly became intense and whilst June would not have expected Joe to leave his family, she nevertheless believed that their relationship was more than a fleeting 'affair' and might one day even become something more permanent, as she had no one else in her life.

To her great disappointment, the latter did not materialise and their liaison drifted into something more commonplace over the years, although there remained a certain excitement arising from the fact that they were not constantly in each other's presence. But a major event did occur to change their cosy arrangement: June developed breast cancer, the initial outcome of which was to have her left breast removed.

June was not convinced that Joe's too infrequent words of comfort pointed to a possible resurgence of a passionate relationship between them, and her mood became sombre. She decided that it would be better—especially for Joe—if they stopped seeing each other. She was more than fond of him and would have preferred his support to be more than just a tepid formality. When she told him that it was over, Joe was relieved although he feigned the contrary. In fact, he was all the more relieved that the end came at a time when his company was in financial difficulty and he was forced to look elsewhere for a job. He would take up employment closer to home which would allow him to spend more time with the family.

Joe had not heard anything from June since their last 'Goodbye' but he was certain that she was the reason someone from a solicitor's office had come looking for him. The situation could get very tricky. Joe decided not to go to work the following Monday in order to meet this providential visitor. The latter would be easy to spot as he would come by car, probably in a more expensive car than usually came to his street. Joe's plan was to meet him outside, before he could knock on the door. This is indeed what occurred and the man invited Joe to come down town to the office, as it was inappropriate to do business in the street. But he did mention that there was a will involved and that Joe was the beneficiary. A meeting was arranged for the next day—Joe would finish work early and go straight into town.

At the meeting, Joe was informed that his unfortunate 'cousin'—for that is how June had referred to him to the solicitor in Coventry and to which he now nodded in recognition—died of breast cancer and that having one breast removed was 'too little, too late', as the illness had inevitably spread throughout her body. Joe was silent and respectful during this introduction to his turn of fortune. In all, after duty and other costs, he had been left the sum of more than sixty thousand pounds. A sizeable windfall at the time which Joe pocketed in the form of a cheque which he gratefully folded in two and placed in his wallet.

That evening, Joe enjoyed several pints with his friend Billy. He explained how he had come into the money which gave Billy the impression that his mate was doubly lucky in that Joe's extra-marital relationship had at the same time proved to be financially rewarding. Joe said that the sum was 'around five thousand pounds' as he did not want to foster any jealousy nor let his friend think that he was good for a substantial loan. He had to hold his cards close to his chest, which also entailed opening a separate bank account, as paying it into the joint bank account he shared with his wife would obviously be impossible. Everything would have to be done on the quiet and this meant again getting out of work early to open a new bank account. The men finished the evening by Billy solemnly swearing no word on the matter would ever cross his lips, and then proposing a toast to the "fine English lady who had seen fit to reward his best friend Joe, for his sense of duty and self-sacrifice."

Joe duly opened a new account and watched as the interest piled up regularly. However, there was an issue that Joe had carelessly neglected because he had never stopped to ask himself how the solicitor in Belfast had discovered his address. He had been careful to withhold it from June. The only detail he had once revealed to her about his family was on their first meeting: he confessed that he had an unmarried sister living in Leicester but he would never visit her as they were both short-tempered and in fact could not bear one another's company. June remembered this when making out her will. The fact that the sister had the same surname as Joe made it easy for the official dealing with the will to contact her by phone in order to obtain her brother's address, which she hesitated to give as she had no wish to contribute to her brother's good fortune. After thinking about it however, she decided that it just might be an advantageous opportunity to gain some leverage over her contentious brother.

On a subsequent visit to Belfast, which this elder, and only sibling, undertook once a year to rearrange the flowers on their parents' grave, the sister decided to call at her brother's house to complain about the neglect of their parents' final resting place. She found only Joe's wife at home. After making her complaint and then sharing a cup of tea with her sister-in-law, Kate—for that was her name—looked smilingly at Joe's wife and asked perfectly innocently:

"Here, whatever came of that solicitor thing?"

"What solicitor thing?"

"You know, the will—I hope there was a decent bit o' money involved?" Kate looked around the room which gave no obvious sign of affluence.

"What will? What are ya talkin' about?" The wife sensed that Kate had not come simply to complain about the grave. There must be something more sinister afoot.

"Oh, it's probably nothing then! Just this man ringing me up a couple o' years ago to ask for your address as someone had left you some money in their will. A cousin, I think he said—that's why I thought it must be for you as we have no cousins in England."

"I think ya must have got it wrong… no money ever came our way." The wife was not going to admit her ignorance of the situation. After a brief hesitation she added: "Ya must be talkin' about the heirloom… the clock we got. It's up in the bedroom. Just a keepsake really."

"Well, you know about it then. That's the main thing. I was just hoping you had come into a bit o' money—you deserve a wee bit o' luck. Your life hasn't always been a bed o' roses with that brother of mine." Kate's comments were always sliding between compliment and criticism. She rose to leave.

"Do give my love to my brother. I hope he is well. But please ask him not to neglect the grave. I would go more often but as you know, I am just so far away."

"Aye, I'll do that." Kate was hardly out of earshot when the words "Sleekit connivin' bitch!" rang through the air.

For several days, Joe's wife remained silent about the sister-in-law's visit. This gave her time to carry out her hunt which she began just after Kate's departure. Over the next couple of days, she carried out a thorough inspection of the household, rifling through all of Joe's affairs and anywhere he might just hide some incriminating document. Finally, in his old army box, she found a second bank book. It was credited to a sum well in excess of sixty thousand pounds. She had now found the money but she did not know who had bequeathed the sum to her husband. She took another couple of days before deciding to put the bank book in an upright position on the table, propped up against the sugar bowl, while she sat on the sofa, waiting for her husband. Joe would see it immediately on returning home from work.

As soon as he came through the door, Joe looked at the bank book and then at his seated and brooding wife.

"Ya went through ma things!"

"I did."

"Luck, I was goin' to tell ya about this… I came into some money an' I was goin' to surprise ya!"

"Is that right? You opened that account two years ago! That's already a big surprise!" This time, Joe remained silent. He forgot that the date for opening the account would be written on the document. He looked at his wife and then fixed his gaze on his hands which were trembling.

"I wasn't keepin' the money from ya… it is for us an' the children." He said after several minutes. His wife was not going to let him off the hook.

"Ya hid it because ya didn't want me to know who left it to ya."

"Aye."

"An' who did?" Joe then told the story of June, minimising its length and intensity, and stressing his concern for this woman who had suffered so sorely from breast cancer.

His wife listened and made the unuttered decision that they would talk no more about it.

To tie up loose ends, she simply added: "Yar sister was here the other day. She came to complain about the grave an' casually dropped the message about bein' contacted about a will. She gave them your address—you bein' that woman's cousin, an' all!"

"She's a cow!" Joe looked directly at his wife. He wanted confirmation that they would continue life together. He did not want to lose her or the children. Divorce could not be an option after so many years together. Even in her grave he could not inflict this on his own departed mother.

His wife had already thought things through and had no intention of breaking up their marriage. She had always feared and suspected her husband's infidelities, so this situation came as no surprise to her. And there was no reason she should not benefit from the money. She deserved it. She had already made a mental list of purchases that they would soon be making. Her sister-in-law would get a shock on her next visit when seeing all the changes that she would make to the sitting-room. Husband and wife sat down at the table as usual and had dinner with their children.

From his wife's behaviour to him, it quickly became obvious to the husband that there was going to be no change to their marital status. That evening, Joe did not go to the pub but instead sat back in his armchair with a tumbler of whiskey and allowed himself to think of June. He was grateful to her for the money and also sorry that she had chosen to suffer alone. Then it occurred to him that she had done it on purpose: she had left him the money so that their relationship would not remain eternally in the shadows. It was her way of making a statement—that after all, 'they' had existed and it was important that their relationship be recognised as such. After all, they had shared a lot of tender moments and it was not just a seedy affair. Joe smiled at the thought. It occurred to him that June was a very intelligent and independent woman but he was relieved that those days were now part of a distant and harmless past.

The Trench Coat

The four boys all came from the three streets running off Stroud Street and were keen to escape the heat of the concrete slabs and melting pools of tarmac on this first, really intense day of summer. The group of boys was basically 'three plus one' as the youngest, Polo, was kept at a distance by the others. He was physically very slow and not a good climber. At the age of almost twelve, he still went to Sunday school and the Monday Night Mission in Welwood Street which the others had long ago abandoned. There was a feeling amongst the others that he was not really to be trusted with important information.

The other three—Spud, Don and Cheesey were much bouncier and more fearless, and hardly went to school at all, never mind Sunday school. Spud was the self-appointed leader. He was fourteen and taller than the others so that no one dared to challenge him. He rarely made suggestions but always made the decisions. Today after considering several possibilities put forward, the decision taken was to go to the Botanic Gardens, or 'Gardies' as they called this oasis of greenness, full of dens where they could forage for objects of interest, and eventually pillage.

They set off in the middle of the afternoon heat and were soon making their way enthusiastically up Botanic Avenue, bobbing in and out of trees; pulling at cigarette machine drawers; trying to ransack the inside of phone boxes; indeed, prodding or poking at anything which suggested the slightest interest or gain. There was no real attempt to damage anything—no attempt to avoid damage either—they were just guided by a malicious playfulness.

When they began playing 'Follow my leader,' Polo fell to the back so that his slow clumsiness would not be noticed by the others and would not be a hindrance to them. Sometimes he would skip any dangerous bits like jumping gate pillars, and catch the others up by running round these obstacles. He was fooling no one, but his actions supported the pretence that he was an accepted member of their gang. Spud went along with this because Polo had good ideas for his age and he could still get away with being considered too young to climb successfully over pillar boxes, bounce on car bonnets and swing from the low branches of trees which lined the avenue leading to the back entrance of the Gardies.

The boys came to an abrupt halt when Cheesey spied a young woman, probably a student as she was carrying books under her right arm, walking casually towards them. There were few people on the street because of the heat and Cheesey noticed that she was dressed in a flimsy top with tattered shorts revealing her very long and white legs. As she came closer, her breasts swayed to and fro under her bra-less top.

"I'd love ta squeeze her tits!" said Cheesey, looking at Spud.

"Why don't ya then?" came the challenging response.

"You just watch me!"

The three boys moved behind a parked car while Cheesey ambled nonchalantly in the direction of the unsuspecting female. As he got within striking distance, he quickened his pace until he broke into a jog. When he came almost level with the young woman, he suddenly turned on her and thrust his right hand on to her left breast, groping her before running on as fast as he could. The other boys gaped, gasped and giggled in admiration. He was immediately established as the hero of the day.

The young woman took time to react but then squealed her surprise before shouting after the boy: "Ya wee bastard! Nothin' but a bloody wee animal!"

The others looked on fascinated and excited, but decided to crouch further down out of sight until the young woman had gone past the car and was on her way down the avenue. They caught up with Cheesey who bathed in the glory: "Did ya see the bumpers on 'er? Big jelly ones!" said Cheesey, still trying to get his breath back while holding everyone's attention.

Jealous of his suddenly increased popularity, Spud decided it was time to put an end to the episode, so he just said: "Let's go!" as he moved the group on towards the side gates of the Gardies. Polo did not really understand what the point of the exercise had been but he went along trying to show that he shared in Cheesey's triumph.

The boys went through the huge dark-green and gold-spiked gates of Botanic Gardens to enter the park near the 'Glass House'. The park was surprisingly deserted save for a few old men and women sat separately like die-cast figures overlooking the vast green field before them. These old people seemed to be absolutely motionless: one or two sat with their mouths partly open as if they had forgotten the end of a sentence; whilst one or two others sat arched on the bench as if they had just dropped something but were unwilling or unable to bend further to pick it up. These figures remained seemingly indifferent to the arrival of the boys and did not stir out of their dumb inertia. To the boys, they were of little interest, no more than suspended wafts of grey, poised unobtrusively in the shadow of the cooler air beneath the trees.

Cheesey quickly looked away from these old people and peered around him for something of significance. He suggested going to the Palm House whose majestic glass dome beckoned through the hot sunshine above the trees but Spud cut him short by saying that it would be too hot inside and they would be better heading for the Puzzle Walk.

The Puzzle Walk or 'Puzzies', as they called it—was a large area of exotic plants and trees, densely grouped and tastefully landscaped to create mounds and hollows which looped into narrow paths with bridges and flowing water, creating an atmosphere of adventure that even Spud, despite his fourteen years, was sensitive to. He led the charge into, and under, the shrubs, crawling through dark spaces whilst ignoring scratches and tears. The boys accelerated on all fours and soon left Polo behind again. He felt abandoned and crawled backwards until he found the slated path once more. He would catch the others up on the far side of the thick clumps of vegetation. He could show them many scratches—some of them deep and bloody—to attest to his efforts. He would climb the hill and wait for them behind the rose bushes. There was a bandstand nearby where they liked to regroup and he would pretend that he had been following them to it.

However, he was mistaken in his choice. The others had gone straight through the Puzzies and were on their way to the playing fields which led down to the Ormeau Embankment. He could hear their whistles and shouts in the distance.

Polo made a great effort to catch up with them. It was not necessary to explain anything as the others pretended that they had not noticed his absence. They stopped for a moment to survey the unexpectedly deserted playing fields. No one was playing football. This was a blow to their plans and Spud asked loudly: "Where are all the bastards hidin' today?"

But he was genuinely disappointed. Cheesey began loosening his jeans and was about to drop them further in order to relieve himself when he heard the park keeper's whistle blowing stridently in their direction. The boys moved on innocently towards what remained of the old changing block which they knew had decrepit toilets at one end. On seeing their direction, the park keeper would conclude they could do no harm and leave them to their own devices.

The changing block was an old wooden and brick structure which was falling to pieces. It was covered with long sheets of rusted corrugated metal which no longer kept the rain out. As soon as he was out of sight, Cheesey began to urinate against the crumbling wall by sending a golden arc through the sunny air. He delighted in scattering the arc in broken splashes against the wall and in the direction of the boys who came too close to him.

Spud pushed Don's back against the shaky edifice and used him as a ladder to get on to the roof of the building. Polo followed, with Spud generously helping to pull him up. The other two managed to climb up by their own means until all four sat on the roof which was much too hot because of the punishing sunshine. They picked their way gingerly across the metal sheets until they reached the space which enclosed the cubicles and urinals. Suddenly, Spud gestured to the others to stop and be quiet. He turned to them whispering: "There's somebody down there. Can yous hear 'im?"

The boys shook their heads and then Cheesey said: "I can hear somethin'. Some sort of scrapin' against the wall."

Muted sounds were coming from one of the cubicles. Spud motioned to them to crouch. Then they followed him slowly and cautiously to the edge of the roof where they sat on the part of the wall overlooking one of the cubicles which had a closed swinging half-door. A sickening odour of urine rose up into the heat of the afternoon and the drone of flies could be heard above the subdued groans of a dark figure clad in a long-grey coat, pressed against the cubicle wall.

"What's he doin'?" asked Don.

"He's havin' a wank, the dirty oul bastard!" said Spud, half-laughing. The man looked up at this interruption and began fiddling with his zipper, bringing his coat across to conceal himself.

Spud shouted down to him: "Ha much will ya give us if we wank ya off?"

No answer came. Instead, the man stepped back into the deeper shadow, retracting like some giant mollusc back into its shell. This encouraged Spud and Cheesey to hastily descend the cistern pipes into the urinal area and then cross to the cubicle door. They waited defiantly outside until the door was pulled partly open, and then they moved forward.

Don and Polo could hear negotiations going on about money and ball-bearings.

"What's 'e sayin'?" asked Don.

"He says he'll give us a sprazzy and a few ironies," Spud shouted up to the two still perched on the wall as he and Cheesey disappeared into the dark of the cubicle. Don began to shimmy down the pipes but Polo remained on the wall.

He decided not to join the others. The pipes were too old and rotten and he was too clumsy to get down unaided. He looked around at the fields and the far-off gates of the park which led to the Lagan river. He was feeling the heat again and thought it best to retrace his steps in order to drop down off the roof covering the changing rooms. It was slightly lower at that end. As he began to move backwards, Cheesey came out of the cubicle and Don went in. He saw Polo withdrawing.

"Where the fuck d'ya think yer goin'? It's yer turn next."

Polo hesitated for a brief instant but then continued on his way along the roof. He crawled on all fours across the rotting corrugated metal until he reached the edge. He then dropped awkwardly to the ground where he fell backwards into the lush grass. He lay there motionless, looking at the sky until he was disturbed by raucous noises coming from the other side of the building. He could hear the other three getting closer to him and managed to clamber to his feet just before Spud, Don and Cheesey stood before him, laughing heartily and rattling the steel balls in their partially closed fists. He could feel a gloating animosity towards him and braced himself for the worst.

"Luck at that Son! 'e gave us two ironies each, as well as a shillin' between us."

"I thought he was only goin' to give us a sprazzy," said Polo.

"It doesn't matter anyway cause yar nat getting any of it!" said Cheesey triumphantly.

"That's right!" said Spud. "Ya didn't do anything, did ya?"

There was nothing Polo could say. He looked at the other three and decided that it was time for him to go home.

The other three boys started out before him on the way to the Puzzies. He could hear talk about a 'bamboo den' which only interested him because he knew that they would not take him with them. The idea of making bows and arrows and even spears was of marginal interest to him but unlike the others, he did not have a penknife to cut the bamboo with. He let them get a good distance in front but he could still hear their talk and knew that he was in part the object of their ridicule.

He watched the others mimic fights: jostling, pushing and mock-kicking each other. When they got to the first trees they swung on low branches, tumbled and fell in the long grass, doing everything to let Polo know that he was excluded from their fun.

Cheesey spotted two young boys with a football entering the park through the Stranmillis gates. He watched them reach a flat, grassy patch where they began to kick the ball to each other. Spud noted that their clothes were relatively new and expensive and concluded that they must be from the well-to-do area just beyond the gates. They would be easy pickings. The three made their way across the field, followed by Polo who kept a safe distance.

Cheesey was first to pounce and intercept the ball which he quickly kicked to Spud and then to Don. The two younger boys tried to recuperate their ball but they were not fast enough. Cheesey deliberately missed the ball and kicked one of the lads on the shin who let out a pathetic cry and fell to the ground. The three played roughly, trampling over the younger boys with undisguised animosity.

The latter pleaded loudly for the return of their ball, hoping that some passing adult might hear them but there was still no one around. The owner of the ball started to cry. Spud walked quietly up to him.

"I'll sell ya yar ball—hi much money d'ya have?"

"I have no money."

"Let's see. Turn yar pockets out."

The boy reluctantly turned his pockets inside out and a threepenny piece fell to the grass.

"No money, eh? That'll do!" said Spud, reaching for the coin. The boy started to cry louder. Spud took the ball from Cheesey and thrust it into the boy's face: "Here's yar ball, ya gurny wee bastard!" The ball struck him on the nose and a tiny trickle of blood ran on to his upper lip. He sobbed into his cusped hand. Polo felt sorry for him but did not move.

The other boy was also made to empty his pockets but no money was found. The three turned away and picked up the path through the Puzzies until they reached the wide open green in the middle of the park, stopping only to drink at a fountain and splashing each other copiously in the process. Polo got closer to them. They were about to climb over the railings to the green when they heard the park keeper's whistle. He gesticulated to them to keep on the path. He was now watching them closely.

The boys maintained an orderly file until they almost reached the gates they had entered the park by. When they were sure the park keeper had decided they were no longer a threat, they turned sharply left into the shrubs to enter the back of Queen's University, and quickly disappeared from sight. Polo was only a few yards behind and, although he wanted to go home, his curiosity got the better of him and so he went after the others. When he scrambled into the university grounds, he was suddenly the target of a barrage of branches, stones and insults which rained down on him and it was all he could do to avoid the heaviest and most dangerous of the missiles.

"Fuck off!" shouted Spud. "We're goin' somewhere!"

Polo suffered from this brutally violent ejection from the group. He retraced his steps, but circled the shrubs until he reached the gates of the park. He knew that he was not, and would never be, a part of the gang. This realisation brought bitter-acid tears to his eyes which he had difficulty to control. He longed for the shelter of his home, a place to quietly lick his wounds. He quickly and determinedly retraced his way down the avenue. By the time he reached his street, the sun was lower and the late afternoon was settling into an uneasy peace.

The next evening, well after he had finished his dinner, Don called round for him to come out and play marbles in the street. He coaxed Polo to leave his home by saying that he was sorry for what had happened the day before and that he did not agree with the others about excluding him. Polo was surprised. He hesitated at first but soon joined the other boy on the kerb ready to play. Don took a shiny ball-bearing from his pocket and was about to pitch it forward when Polo said: "Ya can't play wi' that! It's not fair. I've only ordinary marlies and a stony which ya'll break if ya use that."

Don put the ball-bearing back in his pocket and replaced it with a large marble. He told Polo that he too could get some 'ironies' if he wanted to and then they could both play with them.

"Ya mean, yar goin' to see that oul fella again?"

"Aye, tonight. 'e said 'e'd be behind Billy Crone's shop about eight o'clock. I'll be on me own."

Polo realised that this was his reason for calling round. He felt disappointed.

Don looked at him expectantly.

"Throw down yar marlie," was all that he got as a response.

As they started to play, the sun was settling into a liquid golden light which shot up the blackened bricks of the street. They played down one side of the latter and then back up the other. When they reached the top of the street, it was getting close to eight o'clock. Don looked across the road towards Billy Crone's grocery shop.

"I bet ya 'e'll be there by nigh… are ya comin'?" Polo did not answer but gathered his marbles and nodded that he would follow the other boy towards the alley which ran behind the row of shops.

It was a dark and narrow alley which did not allow the slanting sunlight to enter because of the high buildings. It ran straight for about fifteen to twenty yards before turning abruptly to the left. The boys advanced cautiously almost to the turning, when Don stopped Polo and told him to wait there and keep nick. From his position, he could hear Don's shriller voice mingle with the man's husky tones. Polo looked back towards the road and was surprised by Don's return:

"He says 'e wants you first… go on!"

Polo moved slowly to peak round the corner. He knew the man was standing in the first doorway which was not very deep. He could not see a face as the man was reclining on to the wooden door, with the bottom of his body thrust slightly forward. He wore the same long-grey trench coat as the day before which Polo thought was ridiculous given the summer heat. He must be sweating!

Polo advanced gingerly until he could see the man's face which wore a wide grin where only his top gum was plainly visible. His hands were in his deep coat pockets and as Polo stepped forward, he pulled the sides of the coat apart to reveal his dangling sex. The boy froze.

"Well? Come on!" came the rough, husky voice. Since the boy still did not move, the man pulled him forward by grabbing his hand which he placed directly on to his sex. Polo felt the swollen, tubular flesh. An odour of fish, mixed with sweat, arose from inside the long-grey coat. He recoiled in horror. Before the man could react, the boy fled back round the corner.

"I'm not doin' anymore!" he said to Don. "I'm away home."

"Don't go home! Stay at the end of the entry and keep nick, okay?"

Polo nodded agreement as he walked to the corner of Billy Crone's shop. He looked up and down the road but there was no one in sight. The sun had fallen further but still lit up the façade of the building, sending shafts of coloured light through the shop windows that lined the road. The sun was warm and reassuring. He crouched down and closed his eyes.

"Whad are ya doin'?" came Don's surprised voice. "Yar supposed to be keepin' nick!"

"I was. I just closed my eyes for a few seconds."

Don shook his head. He pulled his hand from his pocket and gave Polo two bright, shiny ball-bearings.

"Ya don't deserve them 'cause ya didn't do much."

"Ya can keep them," he said, thrusting them back towards the other boy.

"He gave me 3d as well—I'm keepin' that!"

Polo closed his hand again over the smooth roundness of the ironies. They partly deformed his clenched fist.

"I'm goin' home," was all he said before crossing the road obliquely to the top of his street. He watched Don walk off in the opposite direction, opening his hand to reveal the silver ironies which reflected the sun into his eyes and made him squint. He turned his back to the sun to peruse them as he clunked them together to make a muffled, metallic sound in his palm. He stared at them as if he could not fathom their relevance, as if they had suddenly taken on a different meaning which seemed peculiarly evil to him.

The boy walked slowly towards his house. The sun had finally sunk and he looked upwards to see fine lines of cloud pulled thinner by the last thores of intense light. The sky was shot with many colours.

When he reached the iron grid of the street sewerage, Polo stopped and looked once more at the smooth metal balls in his hand.

"It smelt of sweaty fish in that big coat!" he said out loud. "And it looked like an eel!" He hated the sliminess of eels. They reminded him of snakes.

The grid was partially clogged with hardened muck but he stood vertically over one of the few gaps. He let the silver balls slip through his fingers and watched as they fell between the bars. 'Plop! Plop!' they went, as they plunged into the dirty water below. The sounds made him chuckle. Satisfied with what he had just done, Polo walked off triumphantly towards his house.

The Good Son

Sonny Williams was in his early fifties and now lived alone for the first time, in the same street he was born into. He had never known any other home than this two-up-two-down Belfast house which they had made comfortable enough for two people. His mother died just over a month previously and he was still in the process of making friends with his solitude. It was a tiresome process during which he slept a lot, especially in the early evening, just before the dusk descended and the street lights came on. It was easier at that moment to let go of existence.

Sonny had taken care of his mother for almost twenty years—ever since she had become confined to a wheelchair. He left his job to take up part-time work in the Ormo bakery to devote more time to her, and he never married. The latter decision was not a difficult one as sexual contact proved to be a shameful embarrassment to him. Other people thought he was a wonderful and selfless man, willing to forego the pleasures of founding his own family in order to take care of his poor mother. He enjoyed that vision of things, even though he knew it was greatly fictitious.

Sonny had had several girlfriends over the years without ever getting deeply involved with anyone. There was pressure to marry—even his mother would have wanted that for her son but he could never commit to anyone other than his mother. There had been one girl he had cared deeply for and, when all the others faded into a single blurred entity, she always came back to him. Her name was Joy, and she had lived opposite him for the first twenty years of their lives. They had played and grown up together and neighbours saw them as an obvious match. Joy had long-black-curly hair which, as they grew into adolescence, he loved to come close to and smell discreetly. He could drift off on the musky odours of her hair. But apart from holding her hand, Sonny never dared explore any other part of her body. Joy was convinced that he would never try. In the end, she met someone at a dance when she was twenty, they got married and moved to the outskirts of Belfast. The marriage pushed Sonny closer to his mother, and when she could no longer walk, he clung to the sturdy wheelchair in which he transported her frail body. Today it still stood folded in the hallway leaning against the wall.

His religion had proved his fortitude over the years. He worshipped a personal God he prayed to and talked with, but could not stand going to church. The institution repelled him for he saw only hypocrisy, personal enrichment, and a desire for power over others in it. This was a concern for his neighbours who, on the whole, were staunch Protestants and would hear no blasphemy against the true, reformed church. His mother also worried about his seeming lack of faith but he reassured her with his prayers and participation in local Christian events for the poor and needy. His religion was finally accepted as a profound, personal conviction which culminated in a shared vision of the next life. His opinions of the multitude of churches in Belfast, he learned to keep to himself. But with the death of his mother, Sonny was left to come to terms with his questionable vision of the next life and the harrowing reality of his present solitude. He had no answers and no solace.

Sonny sat in his faded armchair in front of the made-up but unlit fire. The room was darkening as the natural light began to wane. The street lights would soon come on. He disliked the bleary light given by the neon tubes perched on concrete posts and much preferred the old gas lamps with their popping and wheezing noise which gave out a gentler and more humane light from their stumpy iron crucifix.

"I'm just old-fashioned," he murmured to himself as he closed his eyes. Before he drifted into slumber, his eyelids registered the switched-on brightness of the street lights which made him feel uncomfortable as their cold light shafted the living-room. Sonny shuddered and opened his eyes to see the prepared fire with its twisted coils of newspaper, sticks and anthracite. He was tempted to light it but then fell back into his armchair. It was not worth the effort to do so—perhaps he would never light it again.

Instead, he sunk into the upholstered warmth of the armchair and let himself lapse into reverie. His surroundings slowly faded as his mind slid through time until he saw himself under the old lamplight which spluttered and coughed as it struggled to maintain the flame. He saw Joy standing before him in the warm light. Her hair was as black and shiny as the coal on the fire. He wanted to touch it and he believed that Joy wanted to be touched but he just stood silent and admired the deep blackness, sheened with blue, by the street lamp. They were both smiling, static, framed forever in his mind.

Sonny stirred in his chair but remained unconscious of the room he was sitting in.

"I should have caressed her hair—it might have changed my life!" he complained softly to himself. "God! She had such beautiful hair!" and he saw her once more standing under the lamp, as he buried his head deeper into the time-worn hollow in the armchair. "I should have…" but the image quietly faded until the man found himself again the victim of an acute sense of loss. "Why did she abandon me? Why do they abandon me?" The questioning pulled Sonny from his reverie and plunged him back into the cold light of the tiny room. He saw that the world was getting much darker outside. He pulled a blanket from the table beside him and spread it over his legs. He sat rooted, like an old man who cannot decide what he should do next.

"I must be strong!" he said to himself as his eyes now adjusted to his surroundings and objects took on their familiar shapes. Since the death of his mother, he had become almost afraid of the dark again. He smiled bitterly at this childish regression and convinced himself that he must learn to come to terms with the dark, to tame the darkness that his life was relentlessly moving into. He pulled the blanket up and crossed his legs beneath. He sighed deeply in his newly-created cocoon and was glad he had refrained from putting the light on.

He turned his head sideways and buried his nose in the worn, velvet upholstery. He breathed deeply and became aware of an odour which was unmistakably that of his mother. He would often add cushions and lift her into this armchair on cold evenings to keep her away from the draughts. From the depths of the threadless fabric came her perfume of faded rose petals. He let himself drift again, this time into his mother's arms. He saw himself walking by her side, wrapped in her coat, with her right arm extended to support and protect him. As the years went by, he realised that they had simply changed places and that he supported and protected her from the outside world. Now, there was nothing left.

"Perhaps I should have had children," he said to himself, as he slowly opened his heavy eyes. He looked at the mantlepiece and thought about smoking his pipe but he just could not be bothered to pull himself out of his warm nest. The world around him was too cold and too empty.

"I'll have to pull myself together! I can't go on like this!" he whispered bitterly. He was too old to go dancing and the sort of clubs which existed these days held no attraction for him.

"Full of idiots and bigots!" He thought about moving house. The surrounding streets held nothing for a man like himself.

"I should have gone to Canada when I had the chance. And taken my mother with me." He quickly realised Canada was not the path to follow now as it only added bitterness and regret to his emptiness.

As Sonny sat on in silent dejection, wondering what his next move could be, there came the sound of voices coarsely mingling and cutting into one another. The noise slowly increased in volume until it paused outside his front door. There was no knock, just a continual slur that told him the speakers were obviously drunk. He listened intently and could now distinguish two voices uttering broken bits of sentences, phrases punctuated by incoherent fragments and foul language spluttered out with particular emphasis and vehemence.

"… catch the fucker… 'e thinks 'e can do me outa a tenner… catch the cunt an' knock his fuckin' ballocks in…" The speaker seemed to be almost out of breath. The voice sounded familiar but Sonny thought mainly about the old ladies living in the house next door who would be frightened and upset on hearing these abominations.

The second voice picked up the thread: "Yar right, 'e's a cunt! It's nat the first time the bastard has tried t' do us—ya remember those tracksuits? We'll catch him and cut his fuckin' throat." Both men began to talk at the same time until only the swear words were audible through the running slur of the conversation.

"They're pissed!" said Sonny contemptuously, moving closer to the window in an attempt to see who the authors of such filth were. One man had his arm around the other who was propping himself up against Sonny's front door. He could see part of the nearest man's profile and recognised him as the youngest of two brothers who lived in the next street.

"The MacPhersons, aye, that's who they are!"

The brothers had a reputation for thieving, intimidation, and all sorts of underhand dealings. They were now part of that generation which had come to rule the streets of Belfast and had lost all sense of decency and restraint. Sonny pulled back from the window. He knew it was better not to get involved, if he could avoid it.

He stood listening to the laboured conversation continuing outside his front door. One of the brothers seemed to be getting increasingly incensed for his voice rose in pitch as he uttered threats and profanities. His back was against the front door and Sonny could hear his buckled leather jacket scrape against the wood and the sole of his shoe slip down the bottom panel. It annoyed him that the paint on the door would probably be scraped and need some touching up now.

Sonny removed the folded wheelchair from the small hallway in order to position himself behind the door in the hope that the men would be coming to the end of their conversation and about to continue down the street. He listened to the heavy breathing. They gave no indication that they were about to move on. The swearing was getting louder and Sonny could not understand why no one else was coming out to tell them to clear off. He would have to do it himself, but nicely.

Sonny quietly took the snib off the door and gently opened it, but despite his precautions, the person leaning against it was taken by surprise and fell heavily backwards. Sonny made an effort to catch him but the man's massive frame hit the ground with a thud so that he found himself flat on his back, looking up in rage at Sonny.

"I'm very sorry ya fell… let me help ya get up…" As Sonny bent forward to help the man, the boot of the figure standing in front of him came crashing into the side of his head and Sonny fell backwards and through the flimsy inner door to find himself spread out on the floor of his own sitting-room. His right ear began bleeding on to the carpet.

The other man had now struggled to his feet and both brothers staggered into the sitting-room.

"Who the fuck are you?" asked the younger man as his boot again struck Sonny on the side of the head.

"Are ya deaf? I ast ya a question!" and again the boot came smashing into the prostrate body. Both men now lashed out indiscriminately into the body on the floor. Sonny instinctively pulled his legs up into a foetal position but the men went on lashing out and stamping on him until they were exhausted by their efforts. The elder of the two tried to lean against Sonny's armchair but his drunken weight forced it on its side and he broke part of it as he followed it to the ground. His brother helped him to his feet again.

The two men stood for a moment to observe Sonny's motionless body. The face was already swollen and disfigured and a trickle of red seeped into the thick carpet. They knew it was time to clear off. They listened for any other presence and surveyed the rest of the room in the hope of finding something of value. They spied Sonny's wallet on the mantlepiece where it sat beside his pipe. There were also a few pound notes under a candlestick: "That'll do us for a few pints!" The men exchanged smiles and left as quickly as they could, stepping over the inert frame of the older man.

Sonny lay unconscious for several minutes. When he opened his eyes, it took some time before he adjusted to the shadowy outlines of the room. He did not feel pain—just a numbness which had set into his limbs and ran through his body. He felt the wetness of his blood beneath his ear and cheek but it did not rouse him to sit up. It was his life seeping out, a draining of his body and his will. He was not against the outcome and lapsed once again out of consciousness until he heard his mother's voice and could see her bending over him, caressing his wavy hair. It made him smile and relax.

"Dear God, what's he smiling at?" asked Mrs Neville from two doors up. She tried to lift his head but was shocked by the sight of so much blood and gently rested it again on the carpet.

"God help 's! God love ya Son!" was all she could say. Another neighbour called for an ambulance but Mr Jameson from across the street, had already gone to the local pub to call the emergency services. He returned almost at the same time as the ambulance arrived from the City Hospital.

Mr Jameson had heard the violent exchanges outside the door but kept from 'interfering'. He had seen the two men come out of the house and went over as soon as they had turned the corner. He had recognised the brothers. He now watched in silence as the ambulancemen lifted Sonny on to a stretcher and placed him in the vehicle. Sonny was still smiling, which caused those present to look at one another in complete bewilderment.

Sonny remained in hospital for more than a week. His life was seemingly no longer in danger but the doctors were concerned at his total lack of progress and silence. He refused to leave his bed and would not eat. When awake, he would lie and look up fixedly at the ceiling. At the beginning, the police left him time to recuperate but when they finally came round to question him, Sonny lay stunned as if they were speaking to him in a foreign language. Nothing would make him say a word. It was only because the neighbours reassured the hospital staff that they would look after him, that the doctors agreed to discharge him. Nevertheless, the hospital would keep him under medical observation through regular home visits.

The neighbours set up a bed for Sonny in the sitting-room, partly out of convenience and partly because he could see the activity in the street which would be a centre of interest for him. However, they soon realised that the street was of no interest to him. Many people visited the patient but he said very little and they left with the conviction that he was not on the road to recovery. Sometimes, he fell asleep in their company and they looked on as his eyes moved frantically beneath the eyelids. Some sort of fierce struggle was taking place during his unconscious state but this was the only activity they could observe. He still hardly ate anything.

One of his regular visitors was Mr Jameson, who had informed the police that he had seen two men leaving Sonny's house before he had found his neighbour lying on the floor, but he did not tell them that he knew who the assailants were. He hoped that Sonny would inform them and he did not understand why the latter still remained silent. Mr Jameson waited until he found himself alone with the victim to broach the subject.

"Tell 's this Sonny… did ya recognise yar attackers?" Sonny turned his head away from his neighbour and looked at the mantlepiece. He said nothing.

"I think I recognised them. It was the MacPherson brothers that gave ya the kickin', wasn't it?"

Sonny closed his eyes. He had no interest in answering. In fact, he had no interest in continuing his life. In a paradoxical way, he was happy that he felt weaker—it helped him to drift away from his surroundings. He at last knew where he was going and this brought a smile back to his face.

Mr Jameson observed the patient closely. He saw that his chest had stopped moving and so bent over to check his heartbeat. His strange neighbour had left this world. He waited for a few minutes and then rose to fetch the women who had been looking after Sonny. They confirmed the death and immediately began preparations for the formalities which would have to be accomplished before the police arrived. Mrs Neville noticed the smile on Sonny's face: "Dear God, he's still smilin'! Kicked to death an' still smilin'!"

Mr Jameson suspected that the kicking was only the catalyst for Sonny's death, but he made no comment and simply stood watching the others in silence. He left before the police arrived. He needed a pint.

He walked down the street towards one of the corner bars where he could drink discreetly. It was getting dark but many people were still going about their business in the early evening. When he walked into the pub, he was shocked to recognise two men propped up against the counter. It was the MacPherson brothers. He quickly turned on his heels and left the pub. But it was too late—he too had been recognised in the large bar mirror. The brothers were intrigued by his speedy exit and the elder one came quickly after him.

"Hey you! You're Jameson, aren't ya? Ya live half-way up that street, don't ya?" He nodded in the direction of the street Mr Jameson had just come from.

The brother then came right up to him, thrusting his face forward menacingly. Mr Jameson stepped back. He tried not to show his fear.

"Aye, I know who ya are an' where ya live… ya know what I mean?" Mr Jameson could not move. Petrified, he was riveted to the spot. He looked at the other man and nodded his head sheepishly.

"Aye, you know what I mean!" said the brother triumphantly as he turned to go back to the pub. The older man now needed a wee whiskey as well as a pint. He walked briskly up the street towards the nearest pub on the Donegall Road.

The Romper Room Kids

'God is great. God is good. Let us thank him for our food.'
—Romper Room Prayer

"D'ya know who that is standin' at the bar?"

"Naw, can't make out his face too well from here." Both men sat looking in the bar mirror at the reflection of the solitary figure shaking an empty pint glass towards the barman.

"When he turns around ya'll know who he is." The brothers sat in silence until the man was served, put his beer on the counter, and then turned to go quickly to the bathroom.

"Is that not yer man Digsby—'Digger' Digsby?"

"Aye, that's him, Scumbeg!"

"Wasn't he the one involved in that killin' in Hunter Street."

"So that news even got as far as Australia, did it? Bad news gets around. He was just a glorified errand boy for the Paras. Piece o' shite!"

"I heard he did a couple o' years in the Maze."

"Three, his claim to fame in life is for hoodwinkin' a six-year old girl. Pathetic excuse of a human bein'!"

"Tell 's how that came about—the story we gat was that it was all about food parcels, or somethin' like that."

"Nothin' really to do wi' food parcels. Just friggin' jealousy, if ya ask me. She was a nice-lookin' girl but apparently went about flauntin' it—which is never a good idea around here. Plus, the fact that the local commandant—I forget her name—had to show who ruled the roost. From my own experience as a cop, I would also add that some people just enjoy killin', ya know, beatin' the life out of another human bein'. That side of human nature will always remain a mystery to me. The killers this time just happened to be teenage girls."

The elder brother paused for a moment to reflect, and then went on: "Well, I suppose indirectly, ya could say it was about food parcels as well, in that the hubby told his girlfriend that his wife wasn't sendin' him anything, while she was getting money for it. That wasn't true—I think he was just a greedy bastard and wanted more parcels. But the girl took it in an' repeated the accusation in a Sandy Row pub. That was her first big mistake."

"She shuda known better. But what exactly was Digsby's role in it?"

"Is he still in the toilet there? He better not hear anything—ya know, they took him back in when he got outa the Maze and got him a cushy job as a park attendant or something like that. They look after their own, even if he is a piece o' shite—especially if he's a piece o' shite!" The brothers chuckled restrainedly at the vehemence with which these words were uttered. Nevertheless, they would keep their voices down.

"He drove a wee blue van an' was told by the women to pick up the mother an' child at the Social Services Office. He spun the mother a yarn about a commander wantin' to talk to her, so they jumped into the van. He gave a sign to the women waitin' in a pub opposite and they all headed to Hunter Street where the poor critter was to get a good romperin'. They saw her as a brazen hussy an' were all dyin' to tear into her, mangle those good looks of hers. They thought it was time she got her comeuppance. But the weird thing is, ya know, they had already let her go once, after a kangaroo court—they even took her to the bus station. And that's when she made the biggest mistake of all an' signed her own death warrant. As she was gettin' on the bus, she said about the Bee's Knees: "Who does she think she is? The Queen?" Ya have to know when to zip it."

"We'll have to zip it for a minute, Digger is on his way back." The men fell silent as Digsby passed them and climbed on to a stool at the bar where he began gulping down his beer. At one point, he caught the elder brother's eye in the mirror and nodded his head at him.

"He has recognised me, but I expected that. I saw him in a club, not so long ago, as he also does gigs as a DJ. Bastard always fancied himself!"

"He can't hear us from here—unless he can lip-read in a mirror!"

"Wouldn't put it past the bastard! Might have learned the skill in the Maze—they do learn a lot in there!"

The brothers talked into their beers without looking up.

"The thing is, that Scumbeg over there could have stopped it all. The wee girl was having bricks dropped on her head—he knew the likely outcome of that. A twenty-six-year old man standin' in front of two teenage girls—don't ya think he could've stopped them? Course he could have! Pockle o' shite!"

"An' the wee daughter saw what happened?"

"No, but she heard what was goin' on. Digsby gave her 10p to go to the sweet shop and buy some sweeties. When she got back, she could hear her ma screamin' and pleadin' for mercy inside the so-called Romper Room an' a voice sayin': 'yar not so high an' mighty nigh, are ya?' She banged on the door shoutin' 'My mammy's in there! My mammy's in there!' but Digsby whipped her away and drove her back to the YMCA hostel on the Malone Road."

"But she knew her mammy wasn't at the hostel."

"That's when the fly man hoodwinked the wee girl again—in the car he told her; her mammy was waitin' for her in the hostel. She got out o' the van an' ran up the stairs, God love her. Staff looked after her but I think that wee girl's life ended at the same time as her mammy's."

"I'd say ya were right there. I can't imagine what her life has been like."

"Doesn't bear thinkin' about—you're just lucky ya got out when ya did, kiddo. Wish I had gone with ya."

"I wish ya had too. We could have built something in Australia together."

"Ach sure, no good talkin' about that nigh. All water under the bridge. I suppose ya won't be back for a long while nigh?"

"Don't know if I'll ever be back. Yar goin' to have to come an' see me down under."

"I might just do that. I was thinkin' about comin' for your fiftieth—if God spares us."

"That would be brilliant!"

The brothers came to a tacit agreement before the elder of the two noticed movement at the bar: "Here, yar man's startin' to shift off his stool." Digsby emptied the last dregs of his pint and pushed his stool against the bar. He said 'goodnight' to Jimmy the barman and then turned towards the two seated brothers as he moved to go out the door.

"Ya wouldn't have a fag, would ya?" The elder brother suspected that Digsby did not smoke. He quickly glanced to check that there were no orange marks on his fingers. A professional reflex.

"Sorry mate. Neither of us indulges."

"Clean livin', are yous?"

"Somethin' like that. We're the good guys—the Do Bees."

"The Do B Specials?"

"That's very funny nigh—you're a bit of a comedian!"

Digsby looked at the exit and then asked: "Don't I know yous?"

"It's been a few years but none of us has changed that much, Digger! You lived in Albion Street and we lived almost opposite ya!"

"Aye that's right, got yous nigh! Didn't one o' yous join the police?"

"That would be me. The elder brother. Twenty-five years in the force, through thick an' thin."

"Yer not on duty at the minute, are ya?"

"No, as ya can see, just havin' a quiet pint wi' ma wee brother."

Digsby turned to the younger brother: "An' what about the wee brother? Where are ya livin' nigh? Bet it's not down this end o' town!"

"Ya know Digger, anybody would think you're the friggin' policeman! Too many questions, Son."

"Aye, well, I'll be off anyway. Nice talkin' to yous. May the force be with yous!" Digsby made a two-fingered military salute to the couple and then walked out of the pub. The brothers looked at one another.

"Always was a slimy bastard! But there's no point in sayin' anything. Keep yerself to yerself, that's what I say. We all have to live here—well, at least some of us do!" The elder brother smiled knowingly at his younger sibling.

"Let's drink up and hit the road. It's not that someone like him has any real influence—I don't believe he ever had any an' they disowned him after the outcry because of the killin'. I know that was for public consumption but I think the organisation is a lot smarter than to back that creep. As ya know though, it's just better not to tempt fate. Good survival strategy!"

When the brothers found themselves outside the pub, they hailed a passing taxi. Before they jumped in, they looked up the Donegall Road and could just distinguish the sauntering figure of Digsby approaching Utility Street.

"I would love to give him his 10p back."

"Ya should post it to him—he'd get the message and no one could trace the sender."

"You shuda joined the police force, kiddo!"

'Romper, bomper, stomper, boo.
Tell me, tell me, tell me do.
Magic mirror, tell me today.
Did all my friends have fun at play?'
'I can see Albert and Sammy. I can see Hettie, Christine
and Elizabeth. I can see Kathleen, Lily and Josie, Maud and
Marie… Anne and Sharlene. And I can see you…'

Romper Room Mirror Saying

Eulogy for Anne

Ditched by the wayside
Stretched,
Partially bloating in eighteen inches of murky water
Soiled arms splayed, pleading that you come to fetch her
Take her to the Bog Queen, compare cavings
Credentials for family reunions.
Her wretched fingers now ringless
Like the vanished lovers and husbands
Who once spawned her belly
Her eyes are not yet pearled, but clouded
By the obscene spate of death-lust.
Fetch her to the Bog Queen!
Let the strands of their hair enmesh
To weave a cosy nest
For her children who are lost
For the children who have lost.

The Purse

Mavis Riley was sixty-six years old and had lived in Sandy Row all her life. She had never left the Row, even when her eldest son was planning to move to Canada at the beginning of the 'Troubles.' She had considered taking her other child and setting out to cross the Atlantic but she had watched programmes on the television about how cold it was there in winter and how people could get frostbite if they did not cover up properly. She was even told by neighbours that bits of your ears or nose could just break off because of the severe weather. As a child, she had suffered badly from the cold when her parents could not afford to buy a bag of coal and the idea of spending more than six months in a harsh winter made her shudder. Besides, she would miss her neighbours too much. If her elder son would not change his mind then he would have to leave without his mother. After months of discussion, that is what happened.

Her husband had died just before the 'Troubles' began. He had worked in Gallagher's cigarette factory and fell ill to lung cancer. Right up to the end he denied that his cancer had anything to do with being a heavy smoker and always maintained that Gallagher's was a great place to work. He had earned good money and was given a free pack of five cigarettes each week.

Her second son was not very good at school but he was honest and hard-working. At the age of sixteen, a neighbour put a word in for him and he was taken in to Mackie's factory as an apprentice and later became an experienced machine worker. He was loyal to the company and Mackie's was the only place he ever wanted to work. Over the years, he felt that he had become an important worker for them, a valuable part of all the machines under his control. Like his father before him, he brought home good money and gave half his wage to his mother every week. He never married.

Mavis worked as a cleaning lady in the Linfield Mill. All her friends worked there too and they formed a woman's club which met twice a week and went on trips to Omeath where Mavis ate her first oysters. They were three for a half crown in the early sixties but later became so expensive that they were impossible for her to purchase. She lived with the memory of three oysters which she ate with pepper and vinegar. Those were the days! The days before the 'Troubles' put an end to their outings and younger women started forming clubs that were sectarian and linked to nefarious transactions. It was part of the changes taking place in the Row but Mavis still kept faith in her friends and the hope that one day her younger son would get married and live in his own house even if it meant an inescapable loneliness for her. She regretted that she did not have a daughter and would often repeat to herself: *A daughter is a daughter all of her life. A son is a son until he takes a wife.*

Mavis was resigned to the bitter truth of life which followed a son's marriage. It was simply the way of the world.

The eldest son wrote approximately once a month and she enjoyed his stories from the frozen north where people in cities even lived underground during the long winter. He soon got married and had two children which she had never seen although she was convinced that one day her son would bring her grandchildren 'home' for all to admire. That, at least, was something to look forward to as she knew that her son would not return the same boy who had left her. She would prepare to meet a stranger who shared common memories but who had a very different present and future.

Like all the former members of her women's club, Mavis had become a Paisleyite. She loved the 'big man'. He was the stalwart in these troubled times, someone who would defend the Protestant community—a man who was not afraid to say what he meant. He did say some things which Mavis did not understand and which she preferred to ignore. She had met many Catholics in the past and did not really see them as being 'Anti-Christ' and the Pope seemed to be a decent enough man. Above all, she refused to listen to Paisley's campaign—which was all over the news, papers and streets, and hence difficult to ignore—that called upon God and the people to 'Save Ulster from Sodomy'. It was embarrassing that he went on about it so much, especially at present when there was such a threat to the Protestant state. Surely it was nothing to make a fuss about: she did not know what had possessed her husband but once, when they were in the early stage of their marriage, he did try it on her, although she did not fully realise what all the fumbling was about. For some reason, it was an unsuccessful venture and the whole thing ended up as being just a good laugh. But all this public condemnation of the sodomites seemed to Mavis to be incomprehensible and she wished the Reverend Doctor would stop making such a big thing out of it.

In the meantime, her son Mathew grew into a fine, strapping man of six foot two who had difficulty getting his huge frame through the sitting-room door. She was proud of her son for, despite his massive physical appearance, Mathew had a soft centre. He was a gentle giant, full of good principles, if a little gullible. The latter meant that Mavis still had to look after her son to make sure no one took advantage of his sensitive nature. Unfortunately, she could not keep him away from certain violent elements in the community who provided him with a big stick and told him to patrol the streets every other evening on vigilante duty. Like his mother, Mathew was a staunch Paisleyite, but he understood even less of what the Reverend Doctor was advocating. It was important to him that they were on the same side and that Paisley's voice had become that of his people.

Things were going well for Mathew at work and he was given his own apprentice to train—an eighteen-year old from the Shankill called Herbie Walker. The two quickly became very close friends and would meet up on a Saturday afternoon to go to a football match and then on to the supporters' club for a couple of pints. That was when Mathew's problems began.

When they saw Mathew and his young apprentice together, men realised that they had never seen the former with a woman. This was something very odd about him which they resented. He was now twenty-six—an age which made even his mother slightly uncomfortable. Men at the club watched him closely and picked up on his habit of tapping the young man's knee with two fingers when he wanted to emphasise a point to his apprentice. It was a gesture they did not appreciate. On one occasion, when they were about to take leave of one another, Mathew put his hand on the back of Herbie's neck and stroked him affectionately. This was the confirmation the men had been waiting for.

When Herbie and Mathew went their separate ways, three men who had been following them, suddenly surrounded Mathew.

"So, you and that wee lad are good friends, are yous?"

"That's right. We work together at Mackie's. I'm trainin' him."

"I bet ya are, ya fuckin' queer!"

Before Mathew could say anything else, he was hit from behind with some sort of metal cosh and as he fell to his knees, kicks came into him from all sides. He was left prostrate on the pavement while the men went casually back into the supporters' club, knowing that they risked nothing. Mathew lay still for a long time in his own blood until an ambulance that some passer-by had called, arrived and took him to the hospital.

His mother's face was the first he saw when he woke up late that same evening. They would be keeping him in hospital for several days but his injuries were not life-threatening. His organs were intact even though he had suffered a fractured eye socket, a dislocated shoulder and fractured ribs.

"What in God's name happened to you, Son?"

"I don't know Ma. I just got a kickin'. I don't know why. Herbie an' I went to the match an' then to the club for a couple o' pints. He went to get his bus and then I got jumped on."

"An' they didn't say why? They didn't ask ya for money?"

"No. Nothin'."

His mother looked at his deformed and tumefied face and felt that she had a good idea why all this had happened.

"Don't go to that club again Son, promise?"

"Aye, I promise."

The Mother stroked her son's hand tenderly.

"What's this world comin' to? God save us! I don't know."

"I'll be alright, Ma, don't you worry."

Mavis left her son, assuring him that she would be back the following morning.

During the next few days, as he lay in his hospital bed, Mathew had plenty of time to ruminate on the events of the previous Saturday. He could not get the word 'queer' out of his mind. *They called me a queer! Am I a queer?* He was convinced that being a queer was an illness because the Reverend Doctor had said so and he therefore decided to go to the Ravenhill Road church to hear the latter speak further on the subject. If he was a queer, he would do something about it.

When he was released from hospital, he was given the rest of the week off work. This gave the swelling and discolouration time to abate, if not disappear. He would be presentable on returning to the factory.

Mother and son spent a lot of time together that week and Mathew sensed that his mother was looking for the right moment to approach the subject which preoccupied her. As he lay on the couch, Mavis came to sit beside him, gently stroking his forehead as she used to do when he was a child.

"Can I ask you a question, Son?"

Mathew looked at his mother smilingly.

"Tell us this—an' don't worry if it is the case because it changes nothin' in this house. Son, are you attracted by other men?"

"I thought ya were goin' to ask me that Ma, an' the answer is that I don't know. I'm tellin' ya the truth. I've never felt attracted to men, ya know, in that way… but I don't feel attracted to women either. I don't know really what I feel. It's not something that bothered me before. I just like livin' here with you. Is that a problem?"

He looked at his mother with his earnest and intense eyes.

"No Son, that's not a problem. The problem lies outside that door. You will have to be careful, that's all. There are a lot o' bad people in this world."

Mathew told her about perhaps going to listen to Paisley preaching in his church but the mother's antennae went up immediately: "It's always good to listen t' the word of God, Son, but I don't think ya'll get any answers from listening to Paisley. Still, you go if ya think it's the right thing to do."

She rose to go to the kitchen to prepare some lunch for her son—something easy to swallow. Her support for the Reverend Doctor was starting to lose its ardour.

Mathew lay looking up at the ceiling, listening to the sound of eggs being beaten. He told himself that his mother was usually right and that it was best to leave things as they were, for the present. Maybe they should even think of moving away from Sandy Row. Most of the houses were being knocked down anyway. The place was just not the same as when he was growing up.

Mathew returned to work the following week to find that Herbie had been put with another over-looker to complete his training. He told Mathew that he had been transferred to

McGonigle because nobody knew when Mathew would be back at work. The reason rang hollow. A new and much colder atmosphere developed between them as if both were afraid of something. They were both saddened by this. There had obviously been talk—news spreads fast throughout the community. Mathew returned to his machines where he would be working on his own again. He knew he would have to be on his guard and ready to prove that he was a man to be respected. He would have to steel himself to fight.

The moment soon came his way. On the following Friday, after he had collected his pay packet and was sitting alone, about to open his lunchbox and tuck into the sandwiches his mother had meticulously and lovingly prepared for him, a burly figure approached him.

"Here, tell 's this: are ya a giver or a taker? It makes a difference from what I've been told."

Mathew had not really understood the question but he understood that the man was standing menacingly over him, smirking at his own remark, and did not look as if he had any peaceful intentions. Mathew had been expecting this moment all week. He grabbed the man by his conveniently presented testicles and squeezed until there was a pathetic scream heard by all. He then pushed the man backwards and thrust his head against one of the machines, banging it several times until the man slid to the ground.

Others gathered around quickly and helped the man back, shakily to his feet. They all looked at Mathew. The injured man looked at him contemptuously, saying: "You're fuckin' dead, queer boy!"

When he arrived home, Mathew felt that it was useless to worry his mother about the incident which happened to him at work but he was now convinced that it would be better for them to move house, possibly even change country.

Mavis rose early as usual on the Saturday morning and began tidying the house and preparing the breakfast for her son's coming downstairs. He was always hungry for his breakfast at the weekend as he was able to take it much later than on workdays. After having finished her chores, Mavis sat down with a cup of tea and listened to her son move around his bedroom. She decided to go into the city centre once she had finished washing the breakfast dishes. She had several things to buy and would have more choice downtown. Mavis looked at her purse sitting on the mantlepiece. It was getting worn and tattered now but she did not want to change it as it had been a present from Mathew for Mother's Day three years ago. Like all of his presents to her, it was expensive and of good quality.

Mathew devoured his breakfast largely in silence before informing his mother that he would go round to the timber yard to get a piece of wood for the shelf she had mentioned would be useful to her in the kitchen.

"Make sure you take a key as I'm goin' downtown to get a few things, okay?"

Mavis put her handbag inside a shopping bag and set out for Shaftesbury Square. She had almost reached the bus stop when she realised that she had left her purse on the mantlepiece.

"Typical! I'd forget my head if it wasn't screwed on!" she was irritated that she had to go back home. The door was not locked and as she entered, she could hear her son measuring up for the shelf in the kitchen.

"Forgot ma purse… see ya later."

"The shelf should be up by the time ya get back."

Mavis left the house for the second time and began to walk to the bus stop once again. She was deep in thought when all of a sudden, she heard an explosion a couple of hundred yards in front of her. It was not an enormous explosion, just enough to stop her in her tracks and make her look up. It was obviously a firebomb which had been placed at the entrance to the confectionary shop, very close to the bus stop. She advanced cautiously but could not see any casualties. Apparently, the shop had not opened yet and there was no one at the bus stop. Mavis realised that she had been very lucky.

"That purse saved my life!" she said aloud, but no one paid any attention to her. People had gathered to watch the flames which were soon brought under control.

Glad that there were no casualties, and happy with the realisation that the purse had saved her life, Mavis turned around and walked briskly home in order to tell her son why she was not going into town. He had probably heard the explosion and might be worried about her.

When she arrived home, Mavis found the front door again unlocked and even partially ajar. That meant Mathew must still be inside. She walked into the sitting-room and called his name but there was no answer. She called up the stairs and then went up to check his bedroom: still no one. This was indeed very odd because Mathew would never have left the front door unlocked. She went out into the street to ask if anyone had seen her son that morning but no one could help her very much. A black taxi had pulled up in front of the neighbour's house but no one saw anyone get in or out of it before it drove off. She decided to make some tea and then wait until he came back with his piece of wood.

But Mathew did not return that day, nor the next. Mathew disappeared into thin air and no one could tell her how or why. After a while, she tried to persuade herself that he might have gone to join his brother in Canada. At least she hoped that would prove to be the case, even though she knew he would never leave her in the dark like that. He was always different, a strange boy, but not that strange! She lived in hope of getting word or some sort of sign from him. In the meantime, she spent her days in front of the fire, clutching the worn-out purse that now meant more to her than she could ever have imagined.

The Dead

Mr and Mrs Black had been married for just over sixty years when the husband was diagnosed with asbestos poisoning and subsequently died at the unsurprising age of eighty-one. He was cremated and then buried in a small plot in Roselawn cemetery where his wife was soon to join him. Mrs Black had lived a frugal and sometimes hard life, giving birth to, and raising four children almost on her own as the husband enjoyed various stints in the armed forces which saw him posted to many exotic places such as Singapore, Aden and Gibraltar. He enjoyed the freedom of the armed forces but it was never his intention to look for married quarters and take his family abroad with him. The wife preferred it this way as she was reluctant to leave her native Belfast—and her 'cronies'—but the four children resented the fact they had not grown up abroad, although their views never surfaced as their father inspired too much fear in them.

The lives of the children changed radically during the periods the father was home on leave, when the 'order of the belt' prevailed. The two eldest where the frequent targets, particularly the daughter whose task it was to blacken the chimney area surrounding the hearth each Saturday morning. If the result was not to his liking, the girl would receive three lashings of the leather strap. All of the children resented their father but the resentment was deepest from the elder two. The passage of time did attenuate this feeling and his responsibility for his brutality was lost in the platitude 'But that's what men did in those days'. When he passed away, the eldest daughter was tenderly holding his hand as the others sadly, and to some extent guiltily, looked on.

The eldest son became very much like his father: marrying young and joining the RAF whilst leaving his wife to bring up the children. He did not beat his children but his brutality translated into a fierce and intimidating gaze which inspired fear and informed the children that they were always one small step away from physically feeling his wrath—it hovered above them like a sword which never fell but was particularly close to falling after he had taken a couple of drinks.

Mr Black the elder, had always been a loner and there was very little communication between him and his four children. Like the older children, he too, had mellowed with the years which meant that his younger son, Benjy, was rarely victim to his father's quick and violent temper. The boy learned to keep his distance and always remain on his guard, but throughout his life he was very much his mother's son. She bestowed her love and tenderness upon him and this formed his natural shield of well-being and security. This relationship did foster jealousy from the other children, something Benjy, from within the loving cocoon, was not conscious of.

When they were in their fifties (there was exactly eight years between them), the two sons went for a couple of pints with their ageing father. It was a pleasant, if infrequent event in their adult lives but as the beer started to flow through them, they would take turns to use the bathroom. Once, on returning to the cosy, Benjy became quickly aware that the atmosphere had become subdued: his brother had stopped talking and seemed lost in the beer remaining at the bottom of his glass. The father stood up and told them with a smile that he had had enough beer for one day and began to make his way homewards, content to have shared the moment with his two sons.

When they were alone, the elder man looked sadly at his younger brother and said:

"Me da told me something there that I didn't want to hear." Benjy looked at him apprehensively, fearing for the worst.

He went on: "We were talkin' about Gibraltar an' he was tellin' me about the good times he had over there—wudn't be surprised if we foun' out one day that we have a wee Spanish brother! But that's not what got me. He told me that he knew my mother had a fancy man when he was away. I told 'im he was dotin' but he told me how he knew about it for a fact." Benjy's brother was obviously deeply affected by this news. Benjy had difficulty understanding the situation.

"So, what's the problem?"

"What d'ya mean what's the problem? My ma had a fancy man—oul Charlie Davis from down the street, the wee shite. No wonder she didn't want to move abroad! I can't luck at her in the same way again." He was angry and on the verge of tears.

"Why? Why does it bother you so much?"

"It doesn't bother you?"

"No, in fact, it doesn't bother me at all… on the contrary, I'm happy for her! He was in Gibraltar flying his kite while she worked and raised four kids. Of course, I'm glad that my mother got some enjoyment out of life and that someone was warm-hearted to her. What's good for the goose and all that…"

His brother was not happy with these remarks, especially the last one. He thought briefly of his own wife—no, she would never do that. But his own mother! There was something sickening in all this and Benjy was not helping things. He was getting very angry now and knew that it was best to go home before they came to blows.

He stood up to leave but before leaving he bent over his younger brother to say: "Why are you always so laid back about things? Yar always the goody-goody boy, everybody loves. Why?" and his eyes became bloodshot as his temper mounted. Benjy remained silent because he did not have a ready answer. His brother left him alone in the cosy to brood over their conversation.

Benjy sat on, ruminating, turning things over and over, trying to find an explanation for what had just taken place. It was true that he was happy for his mother and it was also true that everyone liked him and saw him as sensible and tolerant of others. Or at least, rarely speaking his mind. Why should this be the case? It occurred to him that the two subjects were probably linked: if he was happy for his mother and he was the goody-goody boy, it was probably because he had been raised by an extremely loving and attentive mother, coupled with the mainly absent and intimidating father. But this was surely true of his brothers and sisters too, so why was he different? He concluded there must be other factors but he had no time to go further into the question today.

When his father died, Benjy was sad, but not overly so—a fact which would make him uneasy in later life. He could not really understand his mother's behaviour after the father's death. She had had a difficult life raising the children and her marital life, when her husband came out of the armed forces, was one full of friction and dispute—at least on the surface. Benjy had once offered to help her with divorce and she seemed to be pleased and even contemplating the idea. At the time of his death, the wife appeared to everyone to be in very good health and her son expected her to live for another ten years, at least. Instead, she stopped eating. She no longer watched her favourite television programs and stopped reading in bed into the early hours of the morning—one of her frequent indulgences. When her son asked her why she behaved in this way, she would only reply that she was tired and that she was ready to leave this earth. He thus concluded that despite all their fierce arguments, she missed her husband and found no interest in what remained of her life. She had decided to let her light extinguish itself. For some reason, Benjy felt that this was unfair, not right.

When his mother finally died, Benjy was in England visiting an old school friend. He had left because he could not bear to watch her slowly and silently let go of her life. His elder sister broke the news to him by phone and he returned to Belfast to find his mother laid out in the parlour, and his brother and sisters huddled together in the sitting room. There was no warmth in their looks as he sat down in his mother's armchair.

The elder sister broke the silence: "She was askin' for you. Right up until the end." Benjy did not say anything. They must resent him, especially as the sisters had to take turns to look after their mother as she grew forever weaker.

"We said 'Goodbye' before I left." He answered lamely, hoping that they would understand something important which must be left unsaid.

"I know. She said ya wouldn't be able to handle it. She was right." The last remark had more criticism than understanding. Benjy just looked at her. He would not justify his absence.

The younger sister came to the rescue: "She was talkin' to ya as if ya were a wee baby she was holdin' in her arms. It made me think of when ya were a wee lad and she told the three of us that we had to take care of ya." Benjy smiled at her.

He was dreading the moment he would have to go into the parlour to see his dead mother. They would expect him to kiss her cold corpse as was the tradition, but he would not be able to do that. They had done it and would not forgive his further weakness in this instance.

He rose slowly to his feet, and the sisters were about to follow him when he asked them: "Do you mind if I just have a minute with her on my own?" He did not wait for an answer but stepped into the parlour and closed the sliding door behind him. He approached the coffin but did not kiss or touch the corpse.

"You know I couldn't watch you die. I'm sorry." The words of the song she always sang to him as a child came to him and he began singing in a very low voice:

He could hardly utter those last words before breaking down. He could no longer even look at the prostrate figure. He turned and went back to the sitting room where, this time, the girls were waiting to hug him. His brother had left to buy alcohol for the wake. About a dozen people would be coming round that evening. Benjy went to his room to lie down whilst his sisters made sandwiches and carried out other preparations for the evening.

Benjy slept for several hours until he was awakened by voices from downstairs. He knew he had better go down and have a drink with the men sitting in the parlour. It was what would be expected of him.

When he joined the men in the other room, he gently caressed the coffin in passing, before sitting beside his brother and taking a bottle of stout. He offered them 'Good health!' which was the opportunity for someone to say: "Nigh, yar ma liked a wee bottle o' stout from time to time—Mackeson's, if I'm not mistaken." Which began a flood of reminiscences concerning his mother. Most of these he was familiar with whilst others gave him the impression they were talking about a stranger. They laughed heartily and drank as the women brought them in food on little plates which they kept on their knees. Other women could be heard laughing and singing in the kitchen.

Quite unexpectedly, the old man on his left looked at his brother and asked: "Would ya give us a song Teddy?" His brother had a good voice and during that day had given thought as to a suitable song for the occasion. He sang 'In my life,' very softly, with special emphasis on the line "I love you more." When he had finished, he sat with tears in his eyes and everyone concurring "Sure, that was lovely!" Not all of them knew the song. They began looking for another singer but Benjy aborted their plan by standing up and then retreating to the kitchen. He was not one for singing in public and would not go back to sit with the men. He did not even like them using his name: 'Benjy' was just for family, others should call him 'Ben,' it was more adult. He moved discreetly to the front door of the house and stood looking down the desolate Belfast street where he was born.

After a moment, his brother joined him. He still had tears in his eyes.

"Do ya know why I'm cryin'?" he asked his younger brother who thought that the question was totally unnecessary, given the circumstances.

"Because of mammy."

"No, because of you."

"Me? Why?"

"Because, all my life I was good to my ma, givin' her money, buyin' her things, lookin' after her… an' ya know what I realised? She preferred you. She preferred you! Yer sisters will tell ya the same thing." And at this point his brother broke down. Benjy put his hand on his shoulder but the elder man pulled away and walked off down the street.

Again, Benjy could not immediately fathom what his brother had just said. He could not believe that any parent could love one child more than the others. A parent might worry more about one child but they would all be loved equally. This was surely true, was it not? And why would a child believe that he or she was loved more than the others? A higher love, if it exists, is not a reward, not a return on investment. A mother's love is not something that can be purchased! And what exactly are his sisters in agreement about?

Benjy stood watching his brother disappear into the night as the darkness thickened. He went back to look through the glass of the sitting-room door to see his sisters chatting and drinking with the women who had come for the wake from different parts of the city. Did they really feel that he was the chosen one? His mother's favourite child? It is true that they had often said things to his mother behind his back for she had always told him the unpleasant things that they had said about him. He had written the remarks off as just silly talk, a bit of harmless banter. But perhaps he was wrong. Perhaps beneath all the sibling love that he believed must have genuinely existed from time to time, a latent enmity had always endured. There was bad blood between them.

Perhaps it was because of that time gap of more than five years between him and the youngest sister. He was an afterthought, an accidental and unwanted spillage during his father's home leave, and then brought up like an only child by his loving mother.

"Was she really talking to me, holding me as a baby on her deathbed?" The poignancy of the scene haunted him.

Benjy went back to the doorstep but there was no sign of his brother. He looked at the concrete of the modern streetlight and remembered the old lampposts which had a crossed bar near the top, just under the lamp, that you could hang a rope on in order to make a swing. The light from the old lamp was much softer than the blinding brightness that now glared at him. He closed his eyes and saw once more the flicker of the old lamplight. His mother stood in that soft flicker. He could hear her call to him: "Benjy, Benjy, come in an' get yer tea before it gets stone cold!"

"I'm comin', Mammy!"

www.ingramcontent.com/pod-product-compliance
Lightning Source LLC
Chambersburg PA
CBHW061525050726
47593CB00002B/667